BELIEVE IT, BUD

Where the Pavement Turns to Sand is a collection of working class, everyday heartbreaks and bad decisions. In a refreshing rural Canadian setting, the characters in these slice of life tales stumble through divorce, debt, bad sex, and boring jobs, but also curling robots, aliens, jackalopes, wendigo, lots of legs wet with urine, and (maybe) sasquatches with an unexpected whimsy. What makes it work is Birnie's signature dark humor and conversational style that makes every story feel like it was your neighbor telling it to you over a beer around a campfire, or at the rink. Surprising, entertaining, grimy and weird.

—Meagan Lucas, author of *Songbirds and Stray Dogs* and *Here in the Dark*, Editor in Chief of *Reckon Review*.

Sheldon Birnie's short stories are pure Canadian mythology. A modern constellation of heroic day drinking dads, Sasquatch hunters, and ice curling champions. Recommended for readers in the finest denim tuxedos or even regular tuxedos.

—Jon Lindsey, author of *Body High*

The stories in *Where the Pavement Turns to Sand* are reminiscent of the writers who made me want to take this shit seriously: Willy Vlautin, Donald Ray Pollock, Padgett Powell. Look, all I'm saying is, Sheldon Birnie. Sheldon goddamn Birnie, man.

—D.T. Robbins, author of *Birds Aren't Real*

This collection of interlocking, grittily lyrical short stories invites readers out past the glare of polite society to the edges of an ever-encroaching darkness. Birnie's Lake Manawaka is encircled by small town landscapes and characters that will not be unfamiliar to fans of Margaret Laurence. But story by story, *Where the Pavement Turns to Sand* tips us over into an eerier world, where the everyday struggles of prairie life and *Black Mirror* weirdness meet. Birnie turns the screw so that we are fairly certain we've gone beyond metaphors for economic depression into certified monster country. Birnie's stories explore the grief, humor, and terror of human lives made both tiny and tragic within the vast wildernesses of time and space.

—Anne Stewart, author of *Angry Planet: Decolonial Fiction and the American Third World*

Where the Pavement Turns to Sand gives us characters living lives of quiet desperation in a place where impossible things—lake monsters, wendigo, unbeatable curling robots, and more—just might be lurking in the shadows. Lake Manawaka is like a Winesburg, Ohio where everything is possible and nothing is real, a place where Birnie seamlessly blends low-key science fiction and horror elements with gritty, working class realism. It's a stunning collection, one of the most memorable I've read in quite some time.

—Joey R. Poole, author of *I Have Always Been Here Before*

WHERE THE PAVEMENT TURNS TO SAND

SHELDON BIRNIE

Cover design by David Wojciechowski.
Some art courtesy of Touann Gatouillat Vergos, Unsplash.

Title page illustration, "UFO over the mountains," by kolbass, Adobe Stock.

ISBN: 979-8-9874654-6-2

Published by Malarkey Books

For Jack and Stella

CONTENTS

X-FILES ON VHS

The living room of Skeeter's shack was lined with VHS tapes. Stacks of shit he'd taped off the TV. Wasn't much else, apart from a couple ratty sofas, one of which doubled as his bed, and a coffee table covered with all you'd need to blaze.

Skeet had every season of *X-Files*, complete with commercials and the weather reports from the station down in North Dakota that aired the show in its prime. Had that fuckin poster of the UFO taped to the back of his door, too. I WANT TO BELIEVE. Got it off a rental shop up the Wheat City that was going outta business.

He kept them first three seasons next to the bank of old VCRs he had wired to the flatscreen that took up nearly a whole Reflectix-lined wall of the shack out back of his uncle's taxidermy shop, behind the mound of broken antlers and the platoon of rusted Chevys.

Seen those episodes over and over, whenever I'd drop by to pick up, or just smoke and kill one of those long winter evenings. Even if I knew just what was gonna happen during those sixty minutes, it beat drinking in the dirty old bar by the highway, listening to Top 40 and the VLTs buzz. Or driving up and down them back roads through the darkness, waiting for something weirder than whatever Mulder and Scully was after to jump up outta the ditch.

Show went to shit when it switched to Sunday. That's Skeeter's position. Bald-ass albino freak, he's big on episodes about the alligator man, the Jersey devil, that motherfucker who could stretch himself thin and sneak into cracks above doors to nibble on the livers of his victims. That spooky shit. Show lost its edge with all that conspiracy crap, he says. Tried getting too sexy.

But me, I could dig what Mulder was chasing. Dana and that deep state shit. Told Skeet he's tripping, over and over and over again. You fuckin know the government's hiding shit from us, bro.

Motherfuckin Smoking Man himself, Skeeter'd just toast a bowl up into the resin-caked 2L gravity. He'd take it down, hold up. Then fill the living room with that dank haze.

True that, he says, hacking. But don't need no complicated conspiracy to do it. Shit. Most motherfuckers don't want to believe nothin. Like those fucks over in the bar. Soaking up the piss. Fuckin tourists, going in debt to scratch the itch from the lake a week or two every summer. Fuckin happy knowing nothin but the sweet fuck all. Makes me wanna puke.

Bitter he may be, but Skeeter's not wrong. Bout that, anyways.

Not like me and you, Skeeter'd say, credits cutting into the opening of another episode. Me, I just nod. It's not like me and Skeet was ever best friends or nothing. But in a way we was too. Not many people around here worth a half a shit. Or anywhere, I guess.

Not like me and you, bud, he'd say. We know shit's out there.

Fuckin right it's out there. All that weird shit and worse is out there waiting in the woods. Shit that show never even hinted at. When you stare up into the night sky long enough out here, away from the lights, nothing but woods and fields and bogs all around, you know you ain't alone and you ain't special. Hanging with a buddy, even one as fucked as Skeeter, blazing, watching old *X-Files* episodes, beats staring out into that emptiness alone, that's for sure. But nobody wants to talk about shit like that.

Better believe it, bud, I'll tell Skeet. Believe it.

GOLF AMONG US

WHEN JAKE SHIPLEY UP AND DISAPPEARED the weekend before the annual Lake Manawaka Golf Tournament, word around town was he'd done a nose dive right off the wagon. Course, nobody'd say as much to his face when he turned up on Monday, sober as ever and without a hint of hangover. Still, everyone kept on talking behind his back like Jake had run a bender. It's a small town. What do you expect?

Me, though, I wasn't so sure. I've known Jake nearly ten years now, and I don't believe he's had a drop in all that time. I just don't believe it. There had to be something else to his disappearing act. Sure, it wasn't like him to make himself scarce, to miss work without notice. Heck, it's not like him to miss work, period, much less at the busiest time of year. So I figured it had to be something serious.

But when he told me he'd spent the night of August 21 aboard an alien spacecraft, I thought, well, I guess old Jake's lost it, traded in all his marbles and bought the banana farm. Gone plum crazy.

Now I'm not so sure.

As we worked our way around the eighteen holes of the Lake Manawaka Golf & Country Club on the crisp, clear morning of August 27, the morning before the tourney got going for real, he filled me in on what he said happened that night.

"Wasn't like in the movies," he said after I'd chipped a shot out of the rough up towards the third green. Jake's ball was already sitting pretty after only his second shot. He'd sink her for a birdie, while that chip-in had been my fourth, and I'd finish off the hole with a double bogey. "Wasn't like the movies at all."

I didn't say nothing. Hadn't said much all morning. When Jake first got going on this alien business I thought he was just pulling my leg. I didn't know what to say so I just grunted, and kept moving on down the course.

"Weren't no bright lights to be seen," Jake continued. "It was dim, warm. Kinda like a fancy Italian restaurant or something. A massage parlour, maybe."

"You don't say, Jake," was all I could muster as I put my nine iron away, pulled out my putter, and gave my lie a good, long once over.

I'd never been in a massage parlour, but I had been to a couple hoity-toity restaurants in my day. I found myself picturing it, this spaceship of his, as we walked up to the edge of the green.

***

Around here, the Lake Manawaka Golf Tournament is just about the biggest deal going. The tourney draws golfers from across Manitoba, Saskatchewan, and northwestern Ontario. Might be a few folks coming up from the Dakotas, even. For weeks leading up to it the course is swarming with duffers looking to get the lay of the land before the qualifying scramble. While he don't really need the practice—he's been the tourney champ four of the last ten years and always in the top ten—it just ain't like Jake to up and take off a couple days before the whole thing gets going.

For starters, he's the club pro and has his hours to put in, and those are doubled come tourney time. Besides, if he'd had some other place he had to be, he'd have just about bent over backwards trying to get out of whatever it was he'd got himself into rather than leave the club high and dry.

Even if he *did* run off for a couple days to soak up the sauce and run wild in the mean streets of Winnipeg, the Wheat City, or Grand Forks, it ain't like they'd ever fire him. The dang course has been in the Shipley family since near day one.

***

"That there's right where I was standing when it happened," Jake said, pointing with his five-iron to a slight rise in the fairway of the sixth hole, just off to our right and up about twenty yards.

I looked at the spot, raised my eyebrows, and waited for Jake to hammer his ball down the stretch towards the pin. Instead, he shook his head, staring at the nondescript patch of grass with a look of wonder on his tanned, lined face. After a moment, he looked back my way with a shrug.

"I was trying to sneak a quick nine in before dark. That's as far as I got."

Jake lined up his shoulders, glanced up the fairway, and took his swing. Sure enough, the ball sailed through the air a dozen feet above fading ever so slightly at the end to drop, bouncing, just shy of the green.

Dang.

I whistled, shaking my head. Jake, he didn't even seem to notice his near perfect shot.

"Weirdest thing I ever experienced," he said. "Bar none, Roy. One second, there I am, gauging the wind and squinting

17

through the dusk, the next, I'm lying flat on my back, frozen in place in a goddamn spaceship a mile above the clouds."

Again, I didn't know how to respond. It wasn't that I didn't understand the words he was saying. It's just—how's a man supposed to respond to such a thing?

Instead I picked up my pace, angling hard towards my grass-stained Calloway. That's pretty much how she went as we made our way through the front nine. Jake kept on with his tale between strokes, and I just mumbled and nodded, hoping he'd change the subject.

"You tell anyone else about this?" I asked him after a while.

"Nah," he said, looking sadly over the rise in the fairway at the flag hanging off the pin. "Better the town believe I had a little dance with the demon rum than think I've lost the plot, eh? Remember what happened to that guy over Rivers way who said he'd been abducted by aliens? Oh boy. No, thank you."

"So why you telling me?"

"Heck, Roy," he said, breaking into a smile. "We're pals, ain't we?"

I liked to think we were, so I just let him talk on. And talk on he did.

"Dangedest thing is why they told me they done it," Jake said at one point. "Why they chose me, of all people, to beam up."

"And why's that, Jake?"

He'd already explained how these aliens of his didn't really speak so much as transmit their thoughts straight into his brain. I was lost on the particulars of just how they pulled that trick, but it didn't seem no wilder than the rest of Jake's tall tale. Besides, if these guys could fly across the universe, I reckon they'd have a lock on making their *parlez vous a ding dong* understood by a good old boy from the backwoods. Otherwise, what was the point of the trip?

"Dangedest thing, Roy," Jake repeated.

Off in the bush, ninth green in sight, a magpie set to squawking up a storm.

"Said they wanted a crack at winning the Lake Manawaka Golf Tournament. Said, more than anything, they just want to play the game. Ain't that something?"

Once again, I didn't say nothing, but as I swung my driver back to take my shot I caught myself thinking that was just about the first sensible thing Jake had said all morning.

***

By the time we wrapped up the round, danged if Jake didn't have me thinking he might not be so far off his rocker after all. Now, it's not that I *believed* he really got himself beamed up into a UFO and roped into an intergalactic mission to win the Lake Manawaka Golf Tournament. That's just crazy talk, but I didn't fully disbelieve him, neither. Not completely, anyhow.

According to Jake these extraterrestrial buddies of his wanted in on the thrill of a hard-fought golf championship on a heritage course. Only their bodies don't hold up under Earth's gravity, Jake explained, so they couldn't beam themselves down and hit the links. They might have eight arms and giant brains, but their bones turned to rubber under our atmospheric pressure.

"Plus," he added, "our air's like poison to 'em. Pure poison."

That, he went on, is why they had to install some sorta radio-transmitter doohickey into his spine that allowed the green guys to tap straight into his skull and, as he put it, "come along for the ride."

Heck, Jake even showed me the mark the installation left behind his right ear.

"That ain't nothing but a mosquito bite, Jake," I told him, though I had to admit that it was awful inflamed. "Quit itching on her, and she'll be gone day after tomorrow."

"They can't quite control what I'm up to," he continued, ignoring me. "But they get to feel it, see? It's like I'm locked into them, and they're locked into me. Kinda like, half virtual reality, half like those dang video games, see?"

I didn't have a clue as to what either of those things was, not outside of the movies, anyhow. I'm an old man, and my boys never got into such things, thank goodness. I just nodded, let him go on with his tale, though I couldn't help but ask a couple questions now and then.

"Why here? Why Manawaka?" I asked. "Why not Augusta, or the old Links at St. Andrews? Why not Pebble goldang Beach, Jake?"

"Can't just abandon their post, can they Roy?" Jake said without missing a beat. "They got orders from the home planet not to leave the zone until the mission's accomplished."

"What's the mission?"

"Never did tell me that," Jake said with a shrug. "Must be classified."

"What about Falcon Lake?" I wondered. "Ain't that in their 'zone'?"

"Dangit, Roy, Manawaka's a fine course." Jake bristled, familial pride firing him up enough to nearly flub his putt. "Dang fine. Besides, they tried Falcon Lake once. Didn't work out for 'em."

We dropped it, and then finished up the eighteenth hole. When we arrived back at the clubhouse, Jake headed for the pro-shop while I sidled over to where my old Lincoln was parked.

"Hey Roy," Jake called out as I dumped my clubs in the trunk. "See you tomorrow?"

"You bet," I nodded. "I'll be here."

"Right on," Jake said with a grin. "We're gonna give these spacemen a ride they won't soon forget."

***

Me, I haven't put my name into the Lake Manawaka Golf Tournament for years now. I was only ever a weekend duffer until I retired. The couple times I did enter, in a fugue state of vanity I'll admit, I never made it past the first round, but I do enjoy the hustle and bustle of the course when competition's in full swing. The past couple years I've caddied for Jake. It gets me right in on the action. Even though I ain't been with him when he's won one, it's a treat to watch a pro like Jake on top of his game. I guess, in that way, I ain't much different than Jake's little green buddies, hitching along for the ride.

The first nine holes here in Manawaka were built back in the Depression by guys on government relief. A make-work project, but she was designed by the famous Stanley Thompson and she's about the best between the Rockies and southern Ontario, though the courses at Falcon and Clear Lake might give her a decent run for her money.

The Shipleys, they've owned the course since Frankie Carlson, the fellow who commissioned Thompson to design the course and rooked the government into paying for her, up and died rather suddenly before the back nine were much more than cleared. Heart problems, some say. Others add that the boozing and the whoring on top of a bad heart might have had more to do with it. Anyhow, the Shipleys scooped it up at a bargain before Carlson was even cold in the ground. In time, they finished up the back nine to be near as nice as the front. They've been at the helm ever since.

It was Jake's granddad that done that deal, John Shipley Sr. He had himself two sons and a daughter, all of whom were quickly roped into various aspects of course and club upkeep and management. John Jr., the eldest, eventually took over managing the books, while Jake's father, Al, got the run of the grounds. The daughter, Sarah, she kind of got squeezed out of the deal, moved out West years back, though I hear she still owns a third of the place, which must put some walking around money in her purse every year, no doubt.

John Jr. still runs the place. Jake's father died more than a few years back. John Jr. didn't have any sons, but his middle daughter, Jane, she runs the grounds crew now if you can believe that. An only child, Jake seems happy enough running the pro shop and beating the pants off just about all who come to any of the corporate and charity tournaments the club hosts each year. But it's when the annual Lake Manawaka Golf Tournament rolls around that Jake really shines.

If there really are spacemen stationed above these empty prairies with a hankering to hit the links, I guess they done their homework when they honed in on the Lake Manawaka Golf & Country Club and beamed up Jake Shipley. I'll give 'em that much.

***

The first day of the Lake Manawaka Golf Tournament dawned crisp and clear, not even a touch of wind. You could taste autumn in the air. Jake was golfing in the opening flight, a 6:45 tee time. I arrived at the course at quarter after six, but Jake was already there itching to get at it.

"Great day for some golf, Roy," he said.

"Sure is, Jake," I told him true.

I was relieved that Jake didn't mention them aliens, but that didn't last long.

We set off in due course, paired with some blowhard from Melita by the name of Johnson. This fellow Johnson wasn't a half bad golfer, but he wasn't no Jake Shipley. Still, Jake fell a couple strokes behind, and didn't look near as in control as he usually did, flubbing a couple putts he'd put down a thousand times with no trouble at all and duffing a couple into the rough. After the sixth hole I couldn't stand it any longer.

"What's up, Jake?" I asked him.

"Nothing to worry about," Jake said, eyeing up his next shot and giving his five-iron a practice swing. "Guess I'm getting used to these green guys being so up in my business."

"Dang it, I'm serious," I said, nearly losing my temper.

"So am I, Roy," Jake said. "So am I."

Sure enough, as we wrapped up the front nine, Jake's game started to come together. He missed another long putt he would have normally sunk, and his drives weren't quite as on the money as they ought to have been, but by the time Jake and Johnson teed off on ten, they were even, but Jake just kept getting better as they worked through the back nine, finishing a modest two under while Johnson choked, ending up four over.

"Told you not to sweat it, Roy," Jake said as we made our way to the clubhouse to grab a lemonade and see how the rest of the competition was shaking out. "Just had to get used to being synced up to the mothership, was all."

When the field had come in early that afternoon, Jake was sitting just shy of the top five.

"Right where we want 'em," he said, rubbing his brown, sun-baked paws together.

Two of the top five were local guys, decent golfers who'd had good opening rounds, but would no doubt fall off as the weekend wore on. Jake was familiar with two of the others, a fellow from Wawanesa by the name of Patches Boyd and another from Hartney way, Benny Blood. Both boys regularly finished top ten at the Manawaka each year. Neither had ever won the dang thing though, and their best years were behind them. The man currently holding the lead was unknown to us, a young man out of Regina by the name of Kyle Esterhazy.

"Could be a dark horse?" I said.

Jake just shrugged, unworried.

***

See, Jake gave up drinking when his wife, Lois, left him. He'd been a big boozer, a real hard-living, good-timing man, up until the day he crashed his Pontiac Parisienne on his way home from the Lake Manawaka Golf & Country Club. He must have driven that route drunk a thousand times or more, but this time he took the corner a quarter mile north of town just a little too fast. He hit the ditch before parking the Parisienne partway through a farmer's fence and upside down. Nobody got hurt, but that was the last straw for Lois. Once the divorce papers were signed she left town and that was that. Last I heard she was living out in Cheyenne, Wyoming, or someplace like that. That was ten years ago, nearly to the day, actually, now that I come to think of it.

The way Jake tells it, getting sober wasn't a way to try and win Lois back.

"I was in a dark place," he's said time and time again. "It was the only thing I could think of doing that would save my life. I don't know where I'd be if I'd kept drinking. Dang sure I wouldn't be here, living the dream, anyhow."

In the years I've known him Jake's weathered plenty of tough times without hitting the bottle. When the Little

Saskatchewan flooded out his basement and he wasn't insured for it Jake never took to drinking. When his father died of cancer and then a stroke took his mother the next year Jake dealt with his grief sober as a judge.

That's why I say it just don't make no sense for a man who's kept to the straight and narrow ten solid years to slip up over nothing. I just don't believe it.

***

Jake kept at it through Friday and Saturday, and by the final round on Sunday, he was sitting in second place. He was two back of Esterhazy and three ahead of our buddy from Wawanesa. He hadn't let up on the space talk, neither.

Sure, he was driving them balls the distance, setting his shots right where he wanted 'em and sinking those long putts like the Jake Shipley from Lake Manawaka we all knew, but if I whistled, or complimented a particularly sweet shot, Jake would just grin and say something like, "Who knew Martians could golf so good?" In between shots, or sitting at the clubhouse over afternoon Arnold Palmers, he would get reflective.

"Of course, they ain't really Martians," he said, staring out across the fairway and up at the blue sky above. "We'd call 'em Glieseans, after the star their home planet spins around, Gliese 832. Course, they got their own name for it. Couldn't pronounce it if I tried, though."

"Is that so?" I said, watching the leaves on the aspen trees that lined the eighteenth hole dance in the breeze, gauging what speed the air was moving at. "You don't say."

Of course I knew Jake Shipley by reputation before I ever got to really know him personally. That's just the way it goes in a small town.

I've been here most of my life with the exception of a couple years over in Yorkton and down Medicine Hat way. Me and the wife, Shirley, we never really took to any of those places so we moved back home just before our first-born, James, came around. It's a good place to raise a family. A decent one, at least, and decent's always been good enough for me.

James grew up, and so did Frank, our second, and they went onto university down in Winnipeg. James moved out to the west coast. Frank's still around, runs a restaurant by the lake. Shirley, well, she passed away too soon. Cancer, a dozen years back now. Since then, I've just kept going, I suppose. A few years ago I retired and I've been spending my summers on the golf course ever since.

I never did squirrel enough away to head south come winter, else I'd be a snowbird, golfing twelve months of the year. Those dark winter hours can get lonesome, sure, but I tinker away in my basement workshop, keep up with the curling on the TV and down at the club most Friday nights. Time, she passes quickly nowadays anyways, and before I know it the crocuses are out and the course is open again.

I never was much of a drinker and I guess that's how I got to know Jake. Not drinking in a town full of lushes, that is. I've got nearly twenty years on him, but we get along well enough. Better than most, truth be told. Jake, he's never been one to string me along before. Even though I can't wrap my head around the idea of aliens from across the galaxy wanting to play a round or two at the Lake Manawaka Golf & Country

Club, I figure there must be *something* to Jake's story about the Glieseans. Why would he tell it to me if there wasn't? For a laugh? No, sir. Not Jake Shipley.

***

Sunday morning dawned cold and gray. There would be no short pants or sleeves out on the course for the final round. Rain was on the way.

Jake didn't seem to mind a bit, though. He was just a-grinning, raring to make his run for the cup. He still had to overtake Esterhazy, but Jake didn't seem bothered by that, neither.

"Any day she's not snowing is a decent day for golf," he said, well-worn Manawaka Golf & Country Club windbreaker zipped right up beneath his chin. "Besides, them Glieseans are hot to trot. They can feel the win, Roy. Can you?"

"Sure," I said, and I did, too.

Jake's game had only been improving since his little disappearing act, and I didn't see no reason why he couldn't catch this Esterhazy. Unless he choked, or the transmitter stuck in Jake's neck went haywire on him. "You got this."

"No," Jake said with a tip of his Manawaka Mohawks ball cap. "*We* got this, Roy."

The two of us lit out for the first tee when the rain started coming down. Not hard, just enough to get the grounds nice and wet. Esterhazy, dressed in a brand new Titleist rain slicker, joined us. He was accompanied by an older caddy, a surly looking guy about my age hauling a set of golf clubs that liked to have cost more than my car did off the lot.

"Howdy, boys," Esterhazy said, with a curt nod as we approached the tee, waiting for the round to begin.

"Beauty of a morning for a round eh?" Jake joked.

"Goddamn delightful," Esterhazy's caddy grunted, and then spat on the wet ground.

"Good luck to ya," Esterhazy said, ignoring both the caddy and Jake's jape. "You'll need it."

"Got a good feeling about this, Roy," Jake muttered as I handed him his driver, just loud enough so I could hear. "We're gonna show these Queen City sons of bitches just what we're made of here in Lake Manawaka, Manitoba."

True to his word, Jake Shipley done just that. He drove with power and accuracy; Esterhazy leaned heavy on the power, but his balls never seemed to drop where he wanted them to. By the time we'd finished the front nine Jake was two up on Esterhazy. The Queen City Kid was starting to lose his temper, but Jake, he just kept on grinning. He hit par on the tenth and eleventh, and birdied twelve while Esterhazy played a dang fine birdie on ten, but bogeyed eleven and only made par with a heck of a putt on the twelfth, cussing a blue streak under his breath the whole way.

"Dang, Jake, you're on fire," I told him, grinning myself after he chipped in and sank her off the pin on the thirteenth green.

"Don't it feel good?" Jake said, pointing his putter up to the sky. "The spacemen are eating it up!"

Jake had a little trouble on the fourteenth hole, a long narrow fairway that takes a hard dogleg to the left after 200 yards. He knocked the ball about 150 yards down, but sliced it off into the rough. It was the first time he really slipped up all round.

"Feels like we might get a bit of an electrical show here later," Jake said, looking up at the dark clouds and rubbing the red mark on the back of his neck. "Signal's getting some interference or something."

Benefitting from a powerful stroke out of the long grass, Jake finished the hole one over par. For a change, Esterhazy was on his game, smacking his shot straight and true for nearly 200 yards before she started peeling off to the left, setting himself up for a straight shot at the green. The Saskatchewanian nailed that one, too, sinking a long putt to birdie. On fifteen Jake shot fine, earning the par three, but Esterhazy pulled out some of the fine work that must have got him to the final in the first place. He got to the bottom of the hole in three swings himself with an amazing chip in from twenty yards out.

"Mighty fine shooting," Jake told him.

Esterhazy just grunted, shoving his nine-iron at his caddy and huffing off to the next tee.

By then the sky was dark, clouds that had been gray had acquired a nasty, blackish hue. Far off, you could hear what could only be thunder. The rain had died down, though, while the wind whipped at the flag 180 yards away, a short, tight par 4.

"Storm's coming," Jake said, rubbing at the red mark on his neck.

Meanwhile, the course marshals were on their radios checking with the clubhouse and Environment Canada on what the heck they should do.

"Think they'll pull us off the course?"

"Nah," Jake shrugged. "She'll keep away. Long enough to wrap this puppy up, anyways."

Sure enough, the marshals said just about the same thing, waving Jake and Esterhazy up to the sixteenth tee. Using a five-iron, Esterhazy smacked his ball up and over the little creek that cut across the middle of the fairway, settling just on the edge of the rough with a clean shot at the pin. Jake wasn't so lucky, depositing his ball straight into the drink.

"Dang interference," he cursed. "Keep losing the signal."

Down a stroke and on the wrong side of the creek to boot, Jake lined up a decent shot just shy of the green, while Esterhazy plunked his ball on the green for a gimme. Jake chipped in beautifully, coming within a hair of sinking it himself, having to settle two over for the first time all round. Still, Jake held onto the lead with only two holes to go.

Thunder rolled over the prairie as Jake and Esterhazy teed up on number seventeen, a 420-yard, liver-shaped monster, and the flag just visible behind a copse of aspen off to the right. Jake took a couple practice swings, stepped back and rubbed his neck again, all the while staring up at the sky. He took a couple more swings, gazed out across the fairway, then stepped up to the tee and whacked that ball like a son of a gun. She sailed through the air, whizzing like a spaceship herself, curving with the course. She come to rest within striking distance of the green, if Jake played it right.

"Dang, Jake," I said. "We got this."

"You said it, Roy," Jake said, looking up again at the clouds and whatever was hovering up beyond them. "Heck, yes, we do."

To give him credit, Esterhazy also blasted a mean drive off the tee, but she did not hold as true nor fly as far as Jake's. He got on in three, and sunk a long putt for par. Jake, as predicted, sunk his putt on the third shot. He walked into the final hole up four with a smile on his face and never looked back.

***

Not five minutes after Jake drained his final putt to win his fifth Lake Manawaka Golf Tournament, the skies all around lit up with a late-summer lightning display that nobody who seen it will soon forget. Once the electric show had passed through, the clouds dumped rain for days. It was something, alright.

When all of the hullabaloo around the presentation of the trophy, cash prizes, and the like was all done and dealt with everyone retreated to the club lounge. I stood there in the lobby waiting in vain for a break in the rain to make a dash to my car. Jake was standing with me staring out at the sheets of water that were just pouring from the clouds. We hadn't talked much since Jake was hustled off the course and into the winner's circle, me at his heels carrying his clubs.

"We did it, Roy," he said finally, so quietly I could barely hear him over the roar of the rain splashing down in the gravel parking lot. "We showed 'em, just like we said we would. Showed 'em good."

"Sure, Jake," I said, smiling.

Down the hall behind us the roar of golfers getting drunk issued from the lounge. Grown men yelled lies at each other about how well they'd played over the past four days, but here I was, standing quietly in the hallway with the winner, the man who'd just won the whole dang thing. He'd just said we'd done it together as though I had anything to do with the magic out there on the course. As though my hauling his clubs around and nodding my head when he worked out a shot had contributed to Jake's mastery of the links in some mysterious way; as though I were anything more than a hanger-on, there for the ride, only to get a taste of the thrill of it all.

"Sure we did."

We stood there, Jake and me, silent for a moment, the lightning still flashing up in the black sky to the east. Jake grinned, and gave me a quick pat on the shoulder.

"Wait till they hear about this back on Gliese," he said, as the thunder rumbled in over the empty prairie. "That'll give them spacemen something to talk about eh?"

"One for the books, Jake. One for the books."

THE LAKE MANAWAKA MEAT LOVER

L YLE WAS WIPING THE COUNTERS DOWN when Rachelle poked her head into the kitchen and hollered, "Kill the ovens. We're closed."

"Alright," Lyle said as Rachelle ducked back out to the front of house. "About time."

The night had been a slow one, for a Friday. Not surprising, considering it was the last weekend the pizza place on Lake Manawaka was open for the season. But still a drag. Lyle walked down the line, flipping the grill, deep fryer, and warming lights off each in turn, leaving the oven on.

Lyle and Rachelle had been the only ones on after the brief dinner "rush" of a half-dozen tables and another dozen bills for pick-up had ended two hours earlier. He'd made himself a large pizza to take home with him, a Lake Manawaka Meat Lover piled high with pepperoni, salami, crumbled Italian sausage, bacon, and ground beef. It was sitting in the walk-in cooler, waiting to go in the oven so it'd be hot and ready in time to lock up and head home. Once inside the cabin he had to himself, since his parents had vacated after Labour Day, Lyle planned to sit back, put something on the TV, and enjoy his steaming pie in peace. Early next week, he'd be back to the noisy hustle and bustle of the city, so Lyle planned to enjoy his final few quiet evenings in the boonies to their fullest by doing a whole lot of nothing at all.

The counters were cleaned, the inserts wrapped. All the items from the deep freeze had been pulled the previous evening for the season's last hurrah, before the summer resort town closed up shop for the winter. Lyle took his pizza out of the fridge, opened the oven door, and slid it in. Then he removed his apron and stepped out the back door for a quick hoot, jamming a cardboard box in the door to keep it from locking behind him.

The restaurant backed onto the Lake Manawaka Campground, which had already closed for the season earlier that week. A gravel lane separated the kitchen's loading zone from the pine, birch, and bush of the empty campground. Beyond that, the real woods stretched out endlessly to the north. Tangled shadows stretched from the full moon across the open space between the trees and the restaurant's bear-proof dumpster, swaying to the rhythm of the wind.

The light above the back door had burnt out a week ago. When he'd checked the storeroom for a replacement, Lyle hadn't been able to find one. He'd ordered more, but they hadn't arrived. By the time they did, he would be back in the city and it wouldn't be his problem anymore. Not until the next summer, anyway, if he decided to come back out for yet another season. Lyle wasn't sure whether he wanted to spend another summer slinging pizza pies for tourists or not. He'd been doing it since he was a teenager. As he dug himself further into his twenties, it was beginning to seem to Lyle as though he ought to start looking for something a little more permanent. Like something that paid enough so he could actually sock some cash away at the end of the month. If he could land something decent in the city, maybe he'd stick around for once. Then again, slinging pizzas was easy money, and he'd gotten pretty used to the lazy summers in Lake Manawaka.

Lyle dug the monkey pipe out of his pocket, twisting the cap to the side as he raised it to his lips. He flicked his Bic, brought the flame down to the bowl of green buds, and pulled the sweet smoke deep into his lungs. Full up, he held the smoke in and stared at the bright white orb hanging above the treeline.

Far off in the darkness, something howled, startling a cough out of Lyle and ruining the otherwise serene moment. It was that time of year, but Lyle was still startled by the call of the wild animal out in the darkness. He spat into the dirt in disgust, twisted the pipe's cap closed, and tucked it into his pocket.

"Damn coyotes," Lyle muttered, slinking back into the kitchen, his heart racing just a little from the start and the injection of THC into his bloodstream. After checking on his pizza, Lyle made his way to the front of house. "Garbage ready?"

"You betcha," Rachelle, a stone cold pro server who'd been working summers at Lake Manawaka since she was a teenager herself, answered without looking up from her cashout. Now closer to thirty than twenty and studying office management at community college, Rachelle'd been in the game too long to pass up the easy money that came with waiting on tourists in the summer, though she'd swear up and down that this was her last summer as a waitress. "Ready and waiting for ya."

Lyle grabbed the black bag full of dirty paper napkins and soggy paper coasters, soiled tissues and used tampons and tossed it down the hall towards the door. Then he circled back through the kitchen, tying off the two bags of wet food scraps and dragging them towards the back. He set them down with a sigh. He'd have to take them one by one to the bear-proof dumpster, or risk splitting the bags open on the rough ground. He'd done that before, more than once. Shoveling wet scraps was about the worst way he could imagine ending his otherwise easy-peasy penultimate shift of the season, so two trips through the dark to the dumpster it would be.

After hoisting the first bag up over his right shoulder, Lyle shoved the back door open. He stepped out into the moonlight and felt a wet drip down the back of his leg.

"Fuck sakes," Lyle swore, picking up the pace in a vain bid to limit the volume of garbage juice soaking his work pants.

Though he knew the path well, he stumbled along the root-snarled ground. As he caught himself from falling, the jolt sluiced the wet contents of the bag, splashing even more down the back of his leg.

"Shit," Lyle muttered with a shake of his head.

At the end of the path, Lyle reached blindly for the handle that he'd opened countless times over the past couple summers. His fingers pushed the dummy lock, designed to keep pesky bears from rooting through bins in resort towns across North America, and his arm jerked the dumpster lid open. When he tossed the bag into the dark maw, it made a sickening squelch upon landing amongst the rest of the week's trash.

Lyle turned and stomped up the path to the back door of the restaurant, where he picked up the kitchen garbage with his right hand before hoisting the lighter front-of-house trash over his left shoulder. He navigated the dark path then, with his left hand, Lyle reached out and opened up the metal bin and dropped the small bag in. As he swung the heavier kitchen garbage bag towards stinking the hole, another howl rang out in the darkness, much closer than the one that startled him only minutes earlier. Lyle fumbled his toss, the bag caught on the lip. The plastic tore, spilling wet food scraps and soggy napkins down the side of the dumpster.

"Goddammit," Lyle said, heart racing as the dumpster lid slammed shut with a resounding clang.

Another howl rang out as Lyle shuffled off to grab a shovel from the shed, as though in response to the clang echoing among the pines and poplars. For a moment Lyle wasn't so sure it was a coyote after all. If it was, it was a big bastard, he figured, and getting closer. He remembered his buddy Skeeter, who'd spent way more time in the bush growing up than Lyle—who'd been raised in the city and only spent his summers out in the sticks—ever had, telling him there were wolves and worse in the woods around Lake Manawaka.

"Should see some of the things me and my uncles come across when we're hunting up north," Skeeter'd say as he packed a fresh bong load. "Bloody elk ripped ass to tea kettle, antlers hanging up high in birch branches. Claw marks carved deep in the trunks of trees, man, all gory and shit. There's shit out there we don't even know about, bud. Crazy shit."

Bullshit, Lyle thought. Just a coyote.

As he was digging around in the dark shed for a shovel, Lyle remembered that his pizza was still in the oven.

"Aw crap," he muttered, abandoning his search and bolting for the kitchen.

He arrived just in time, the cheese bubbling, the crust and bacon strips crisped to the verge of burnt. He pulled the pie out with the paddle and slid it into the open, waiting box with a plop. As he slammed the oven door and flipped its switch to the off position, Rachelle pushed open the kitchen door.

"I'm outta here," she called, poking her bleached blonde head in quickly. "See ya tomorrow, Lyle!"

"See ya, Rachelle," Lyle called back as she ducked out, headed home to her two-year-old daughter and beer-bellied boyfriend. Lyle had always had a crush on Rachelle, ever since he started at the pizza place as a fifteen-year-old dishwasher. But she was a couple years older than he was and more or less out of his league besides. They'd made out once, at a staff party four years ago when they'd both been single and drunk, but Rachelle had never brought it up, so Lyle hadn't either. Still, it was better than nothing, providing a fuzzy memory Lyle returned to again and again late nights and early mornings when he was alone and needing some quick comfort. "Have a good night, eh!"

As the front door closed and latched behind Rachelle, Lyle sliced the pizza first into cheesy halves, then into quarters and eighths. After folding the lid into place, he flipped the heat lamps back on and carried the dirty pie cutter over to the dish pit. Cursing his luck, he headed back out to deal with the mess he'd made of the garbage.

While fishing the shovel out of the black maw of the shed, Lyle was tempted to forget about it and leave the garbage and food scraps where they lay. What difference would it make if a stupid bear or that horny old coyote that kept yowling in the near distance came scrounging around on the last day of the season? Sweet nothing, no doubt. But if some clueless dummy did get hurt, stumbling around after the Beach Club Bar down the road shut its doors at closing time, his ass would be grass. This time of year, there wasn't anyone else around to pin your screwups on. Besides, it would only take a few seconds.

Shovel in hand, Lyle shuffled down the dark path to the trash bin and bent to the task at hand. The metal blade scraped against the gravel at the foot of the bin, shucking into the wet trash. With his right hand, Lyle lifted the shovel's load into the bin, the lid of which he held open with his left. Three, four, five scoops later, Lyle figured the mess was as good as gone. Good enough, anyhow. He let the lid close quietly, turned his back on the deep dark woods, and began walking towards the shed.

He hadn't taken three steps when he heard the rustling of leaves and the snapping of small branches behind him. Lyle stopped, hair rising along his arms and up his neck.

He craned his head stiffly back towards the dumpster and the woods beyond. But all he could see was the shadow of the hulking metal bin in the moonlight.

"What the hell?"

The wind whistled through the pines, the bare birch and aspen branches. The only other sound Lyle could make out was the pumping of his own blood through his veins, racing past his inner ear, pulse hammering like a double kick drum.

"There's some messed up shit out there," he remembered Skeeter telling him on more than one wasted occasion. "Things you never seen, bud. Fuckin things you could never imagine."

"Get it together," Lyle told himself, standing there in the darkness before letting out a long held breath. While he had never really bought Skeeter's line of bullshit, if the night were dark enough, or the wind loud enough, Lyle's mind was known to wander into those dark corners of his imagination. The woods stretched out to the north for miles and miles, broken only by the occasional logging or mining road. Though he was loath to admit it, there was certainly space out there for Skeeter's crude beasts to run amok. "You're tripping."

But as he turned back and took his first step towards the restaurant, Lyle heard it again. The heavy, distinctive crunch of leaves and the cold snap of dry wood. Gripping the shovel tight with both hands, Lyle stared into the darkness, heart pounding. When nothing emerged, he shook his head in disgust.

"Quit being a dumbass," he cussed, hustling back to the shed and tossing the shovel in. He slammed the door and slapped the padlock closed.

Lyle hurried into the kitchen and flipped the heat lamps off. He picked up his warm pizza box, hit the lights, and made his way out the back door again. He was in such a rush that he forgot to sign out before he kicked the piece of cardboard that kept the back door from latching out of the way, slamming the door behind him. Once it was closed and locked behind, Lyle was determined to slide in behind the wheel of his car and get outta there, pronto. Fuck signing out. He'd do it in the morning.

Gravel crunched under his grease-splattered sneakers as Lyle hustled across the back lot. Closing in on his Buick LeSabre, he began fumbling in his filthy chef pants for his keys. He set the warm pizza box on the roof of his car and pulled out his keys.

As he was working the key blindly into the lock, Lyle looked up, furtively scanning the shadows that surrounded him from all sides. The lock clicked and Lyle wrenched the heavy door open, dome light flashing. When he grabbed the pizza from the roof of his car, his eye caught something moving through the darkness among the trees to his left. He stepped back with a start and the greasy box slid from his hands. As it hit the ground, the box popped open, spilling the Lake Manawaka Meat Lover out over the gravel and pine needles at his feet.

"Come on," Lyle moaned in exasperation, his eyes scanning the darkness, hoping to see a lost cat or dumbass dog mosey out of the woods. But nothing emerged. In a quick burst of relief, Lyle realized that it was probably just Skeeter playing a dumb joke.

"Seriously," Skeeter had said after burning one down. "You ever heard of the windigo? Fuckin Indian legend, bud. But my uncles, they swear that shit's for real. She's the beast of beasts, bud. Like, pure fuckin' evil, man. No shit."

"Very funny, Skeeter," Lyle yelled into the night as he stooped down, hoping to salvage some of his pizza. If Skeeter was pulling his leg, then Skeet could find his own way to get high tonight. Lyle had had just about enough of Skeeter's endless line of backwoods bullshit. He took some assurance that once he was in the city, he wouldn't have to hear about wolves or windigos or whatever the fucks anymore. Not until next summer, at least. "Hardy fuckin har, buddy! Hardy fuckin har."

But the wailing wind was the only reply Lyle received. Skeeter didn't come stepping out of the darkness. Neither did a lost cat nor any dumbass dog. Lyle took a deep breath, his blood *thump thump thumping* past his ears, and shoveled a couple slices of pizza back into the box.

When a branch snapped right behind him, Lyle jumped at the sound, spinning around.

"Dammit, Skeeter," Lyle cursed, ready to confront his buddy with a solid jab to the shoulder or a kick to the nuts. Instead, he found himself staring into the eyes of a beast that towered over him, easily the biggest thing he'd ever seen. Whatever it was, Lyle realized with sinking horror, it was no coyote. Skeeter had warned him, on more than one occasion. But he hadn't listened. It turned out Skeeter and his inbred uncles weren't so full of shit, after all. The slices of pizza that he'd collected slid from his greasy fingers.

"Oh, shit," he started to say. Then whatever it was—it looked like a coyote, if a coyote were bigger than the biggest wolf he'd ever imagined and stood upright on its hind legs like an enraged and overprotective mama bear—growled at him low and mean. Lyle tried to force himself to take the couple steps backward into the open door of his LeSabre, but his legs wouldn't move. Instead, his bladder let loose and he began to moan, hot piss dribbling down his leg to soak the dirt next to his forgotten Lake Manawaka Meat Lover.

LYLE & DWIGHT ARE AT IT AGAIN

Whatever it was that happened during the time it took Lyle and Dwight to make it down the three flights of stairs from my apartment, they were full-on fighting by the time they hit the street.

I'd stuck my head out the window to wish the brothers a final "Merry Christmas," and there they were, throwing down on the boulevard snowbank. I stuck my head back in where it was warm.

"Guys," I hollered back into the living room at the half-dozen others sitting around, drinking and smoking and carrying on. "Lyle and Dwight are at it again."

A couple folks crowded around the window to see. But nobody got too excited. Those two had been slugging it out since they were kids. They fought at school. They fought at summer camp, at picnics, at weddings. They fought on the ice during a game once when they were on the same peewee hockey team.

Sure, they loved each other. But there was no stopping them. They were brothers.

The boys were in town for the holidays, same as half the others in my apartment that Saturday night. Most of us hadn't seen each other since the summer, some folks working out west, others in school out east. We were all getting good and lit up with holiday cheer. Why not? Monday was Christmas.

The brothers' disagreement seemed to have started shortly after they mentioned they were headed to the lake the next morning, to spend Christmas at the family cottage, winterized for just such occasions as it was. But it could have been simmering for some time. Hours, days, weeks. Years.

"Seen some wolves playing out on the lake, last time I was there in the winter," I said, or something along those lines. It's a beautiful memory, even years later. Those wolves, two of them out there just prancing about on that thick ice, snow falling all around them. Not a care in the world, it seemed. Or maybe they were brothers too, scrapping like brothers do? "Never seen nothing like it."

Lyle sank back into my sofa and mumbled something. Dwight's booming laugh filled the smoky room.

"What's that?" someone asked.

"Wolf talk's spookin the Lyler," Dwight said with an evil grin. "That right, bud?"

"Fuck off," Lyle muttered, no doubt hoping the subject would change, pronto. No dice.

"Lyler thinks there's werewolves or worse in the woods up there," Dwight jeered. "Says he even saw one, once. Didn'tcha, Lyler?"

"Seriously," Lyle said, seething though he tried to play it cool. "Fuck off."

"But that's what you told me, wasn't it?" Dwight was in his glory needling his little bro. "You said you saw a werewolf. Out back of the pizza place that one time. Didn't you?"

"Could have been anything," Lyle demurred, pulling a fresh bag of weed out and throwing a nug on the coffee table. "Fuckin bear, fuckin coyote. Fuckin werewolf. I dunno. That was a long time ago."

"Maybe a windigo?" someone offered. Whether they were being helpful or piling on was hard to tell. "Bigfoot?"

"Sure," Lyle said, dismissively. "Who knows. I was fuckin high OK?"

That got a laugh, sure enough. Lyle rolled a cannon, more drinks were poured, and everyone moved on. Looking back you could feel the resentment burning between the brothers, though everyone ignored it at the time.

Yet when they left a little after midnight, something set them off in that stairwell. Why else would they be down there in the street, big fat snowflakes falling all around them, pummeling each other senseless until they finally broke it up and stumbled off towards the bridge and the bars beyond, yelling back and forth at each other until they faded into the snowfall?

The holidays can be emotional. Old beefs often come bubbling up from the depths like a bad case of gas. It's been years since I've seen my own brother over the holidays, for a laundry list of mostly stupid reasons. You just never really know what can set someone off during the darkest depths of winter.

SOO-SOO GO BYE-BYE

BABY GAL DROPPED HER SOOTHER in a potty full of piss this morning.

My soo-soo, she says, grabbing for it. But I snatch that sucker outta there lickety-split.

Sorry, baby gal, I tell her as the tears start welling in her eyes. Soo-soo go bye-bye now.

Baby gal, she's not really a baby anymore. She's two. Two-and-a-half. Somewhere in there. Probably too old for a soother. But she doesn't go to sleep without one. I figure, this pee-pee-soo-soo situaish provides as good an excuse as ever for baby gal to go cold turkey on that front this evening.

But come seven o'clock, baby gal's screaming blue murder. She won't quit. Now, who's pulling on their boots and parka and warming up the car to drive across town to Walmart to get a new pack of soo-soos instead of kicking back with a couple fancy pops and enjoying the hockey game? Yours truly, yessiree.

Ah what's the harm, my wife figures, bouncing the crying gal on her knee. I don't argue. I hate to hear baby gal cry like that, even though I worry her teeth'll come out all bucked up from sucking a damn pacifier night-in, night-out for years. It'll only take a half hour, right?

Outside, it's cold, been dark for hours. Even though the car's been plugged in since I got back from work, she still has a hard time turning over. This old Nissan's on her last legs, no two ways about it. But an upgrade's just not in the cards. While she's warming up, I scrape the windows. Once they're clear I just sit, tune in the hockey game on the AM dial, and wait on the heater to work its magic.

It's slow going, once the Nissan got rolling. The Walmart's not far, ten maybe fifteen minutes door-to-parking lot. But the roads are the shits, blowing snow whirling every which way. Icy and slick from the bitter cold, the intersections are like skating rinks in these all-seasons. The Jets have been scored on twice since I left the house. The wind rocks my little rust bucket as I cross the bridge over the wide frozen river. If only the wind would pick me up and blow me far away, far to the south where I could cultivate a deeply cancerous tan and never listen to another hockey game on the radio ever again.

I think of my daughter, her rosy cheeks, her tiny fists clenched as she travels through dreamland, soo-soo secure in her jaws. All this to pacify a child.

My phone buzzes in my pocket. I pull it out. My wife, texting new items for me to fetch.

TP

Wipes

Pads

Chips?

OK, I text back, trying to keep my eyes on the road. As I'm passing this line of big-ass houses along the river to my right, each one still all done up with holiday lights, I catch something big and white lumbering along the tree line.

What the shit?

I blink three, four times quick. The window's frosty, streaked with dirt and road salt. But the big white sasquatch-looking motherfucker's still there, moving from the wind-shield to passenger-side window before passing out of sight as I cruise up the road towards Walmart.

Surely, my tired eyes have deceived me. But I never smoke weed anymore, not while baby gal's still up anyway, and I'm only two beers deep here. Whatever I'd seen had probably just been the homeowner, decked out in some faded coveralls, covered in snow from head to toe. A giant homeowner, maybe. Andre-the-Giant-sized son of a bitch. Or two teens stacked on top of each other, playing a hilarious joke? Surely not some wayward abominable snowperson ambling through riverfront properties.

No fuckin way.

As I pull up to the next set of lights, they turn red. I'm slow on the uptake, thinking about whatever it was I'd just seen, so when I hit the brakes, I'm sliding. Shit bugger damn. Cars are rolling through the green. The Nissan's slowing, but still she ain't stopping. Shit shit shit. I lay on the horn as I pass the stop line, like a slow rock into the house, front end peeling around to the left. Cars creeping through the intersection are blaring their horns back at me as I finally come to rest, well into the first lane of crosswise traffic. A pickup swerves, narrowly missing the passenger-side corner of the Nissan. Driver gives me the finger.

Fuck sakes.

Boy, I am rattled when I pull into the Walmart parking lot not five minutes later. I circle the lot, looking for a spot that's not an icy football field away from the front door, and almost crash into the back of a minivan.

Inside, I nod to the old lady smiling inside the doors in her blue smock against the glare of the bright lights as I pull out my phone and check the wife's texts for the list of what I need to get outta here. Switching the plastic basket from hand to hand, the blood slowly thaws in my fingers, and I shuffle along, checking the items off one by one.

TP

Wipes

Pads

Chips

Candy bars (for good measure)

The whole time, though, I'm thinking of whatever the hell it was I seen back there in the snow. Some sorta missing link type situaish? Bigfoot? Motherfucking Yeti? For the life of me I cannot figure that shit out. It just don't make sense. I'm standing in line for self-checkout when I realize I forgot the goddamn soothers.

Ain't that just the shits, eh?

Muttering apologies, I snake my way back out of the corral and retrace my steps to the baby section. My girl's really too old for this shit. Aren't we all though, sugar? I grab a couple packs, so as not to have to do this again the next time one rips or goes missing or falls in a plastic bucket full of piss. But this is the end of the line for the soo-soo train, baby gal. For real, this time.

Crossing the parking lot, I'm slow and steady against the assault of the relentless north wind. Safely back at the Nissan, I toss the bag of goods in the passenger seat and crank up the heat. I shut the radio right off when I hear the boys have let yet another in headed into the third. After giving her a minute to warm up, I ease the Nissan out of the lot and back into traffic.

But as I'm getting back close to that stretch of houses up along the bend in the river, I can't sit still. I'm craning my neck, eyes peeled, looking through the frost for that whatever the fuck it was to reappear. Passing the yard where I swear I'd seen the beast lumber through not a half hour earlier, sure enough there's nothing there but trees and snow and darkness, house in back all lit up as though Christmas hadn't been a month ago. No sign of a snowperson, friendly or otherwise.

Shit. I laugh, shake my head, and crank the radio back on, over to an FM rock station. Kick out the jams. Bigfoot ain't real, dummy. Every-fuckin-body knows that.

But as I'm crossing that bridge, I'm not convinced. I'm not usually one to buy into that supermarket checkout tabloid wacko-tobacco crap. But what the hell do I know? I work for the telephone company. Maybe there is something to it after all? Perhaps its task is as thankless as mine, and this tall bastard followed the river into town, looking for something to pacify its own squalling progeny out in the icy swamps and barren trees up by the big lake, or wherever the hell it might call home in this frozen world? Whatever it is would probably rather be somewhere warm, wouldn't it? Wouldn't we all?

When I get home, guess who's fast asleep? You guessed it: baby gal. Guess she's been sawing zzzs since about ten minutes after I left the house. About the time I was passing bigfoot, sasquatch, or whatever out there on the side of the road. Whatever it was that was there and then wasn't.

Mama bear, she's curled up on the couch with a murder show on. I shrug outta my winter gear, flop on the couch beside her for a kiss, crack the bag of chips and settle in. After a couple cold ones, though, I'm still stuck stewing over whatever it was I seen out there. I can't explain it any more than I could a couple hours ago. But I keep glancing out the frosty window to the wind blowing snow between our tightly packed houses, looking for that big old white body to come creeping down the road. Waiting on a furry face to peer back in at us through the glass.

I crack another cold one, dig around for a roach I been saving. If nothing else, I'm sure I know who's been doing the grisly string of murders on this TV show.

Pretty sure, anyhow.

GOOD THINGS ON THE WAY

SHE WORKED MORNINGS AT A RESTAURANT just down the street, and on her lunch break she'd come back to their one-room apartment and make him breakfast. She'd cook eggs on the hot plate, and make toast and instant coffee. She wouldn't let him eat in bed because when he did he went right back to sleep after he was finished. She made him get up and dress, and they ate their meal on TV trays on the couch. If she could, she'd bring a copy of the daily paper back from work with her. If she did, he sat and read through the classifieds.

"Anything today?" she'd ask. Usually, he'd say "No, not today." But sometimes he chewed his bottom lip and nodded his head, and that's when she knew there was something. Today there was something.

After they'd finished she'd gather the dishes and stack them by the sink, and he would tidy them up after she'd gone. Then they'd sit around and share a cigarette, and maybe talk about how her shift was going, so far. When the cigarette was finished, she'd go to the washroom, and then she'd be off to work again. Before she left, she'd give him the tips she'd made so far that day, and he'd use the tips to buy whatever they needed most. Toilet paper, condoms, cigarettes, beer. Sometimes, if she'd done real well that morning, he'd treat himself to a Hustler, or buy a bottle of rye and some cola. If there was anything left over, and he didn't think she'd notice, he'd score a gram off a guy he knew at the pool hall and get high before she got home. On her day off, she did the grocery shopping. Today she gave him thirty bucks. She needed tampons, and they were low on smokes.

Once she left, he'd usually sit around the apartment a while, jerk off, then go out and do the shopping.

Sometimes, if he'd found anything in the paper, he'd go to the pay phone downstairs and call about a job. A while back he'd gotten on with a road construction crew for a month, but then winter had come along. Since then, nothing.

It was cold and windy today, and his body was frozen beneath his denim jacket. At the corner store he picked up her tampons and a pack of Player's Light, which left just ten bucks for booze. He walked the next three blocks to the liquor store and bought a sixer of Alberta Genuine Draft, which left him with a pocket full of change. They saved the change from her tips in an empty sixty of JD beside the bed. When it filled up, they'd empty it, roll the coins, and take them to the bank. Usually, the money went to paying overdue bills, but once they were in the clear, they used the cash to get a couple ounces, which she'd sell to coworkers. He'd sell to friends of his younger brother, kids still in high school who didn't know any better if he shorted them. They'd make their money back, and he'd smoke for free for a month or so.

Sixer under his arm, tampons and smokes in the pockets of his jacket, he started walking back to the apartment. Halfway there, an old Lincoln Town Car pulled up next to him. Tony leaned across the seat and opened the door. He hopped in.

"How's she goin, Tony?" he said. He and Tony had grown up together, their mothers having been best friends in high school and having both gotten pregnant their final year.

"Not so bad, bud," Tony said. "Headed home?"

"Yup."

"Anything goin on today?"

"Nope."

"Wanna make some money?"

"Hell yes."

Ever since they were sixteen or seventeen, Tony'd been one of those guys who could find easy money. Once he found out how to get into the music room of the little Baptist private school on the hill after hours. They went by after dark one night and made off with the PA and another grand worth of musical equipment. Another time, he'd gotten them into a big auto parts shop, and they made off with nearly ten grand in gear. Tony also knew how to find people who would pay for the stuff. Sometimes, Tony'd need a hand.

"Right on."

"Anything special?"

"Not really," Tony said. "But she'll pay."

Tony went on to explain the plan, which involved a shipment of snowmobile parts being delivered to the Yamaha dealership that evening, and how, if they worked it just right, they could make off with a good haul.

"I can throw you $500," Tony said. "Maybe a little extra, see how she goes."

"I'm in," he told Tony.

"Beauty," Tony said, pulling up to the apartment block. "Pick you up at eleven."

"Sure thing."

***

When her shift was over at two that afternoon, she came home and they had a beer together. Over a smoke, he told her about the job Tony'd lined up. While she worried about Tony and the job, she was glad he was doing something. The cash would cover the bills, and some of the interest that was piling up, too.

"Don't worry," he'd say every time. "Tony knows what he's doing."

"Yeah," she'd say, and that would be the end of it. If they talked about it anymore, it'd make them both nervous and probably they'd fight, so they just let it be.

Sometimes, in the afternoons, after her shift and the beers and the smokes were finished, they'd get it on and then nap a while. Somewhere around five, she'd fix something, usually consisting of frozen veggies, potatoes, some instant pasta or soup. Sometimes they'd head down to the diner before it closed up. But even with her getting half price, it was still costly. Tonight, they splurged on the diner, and he had a steak sandwich, while she had fried chicken.

Tony picked him up at eleven. They parked his car a block from the Yamaha dealer, and when the time was right, he made the move, Tony waiting behind the wheel. When he gave the signal ten minutes later, Tony pulled up into the shadows and they made off with a trunk full of parts. Two days later, Tony swung by his place with $800 cash.

"Good work, buddy," Tony said.

"Fuckin eh," he said, grinning like a fool.

Five hundred went right to rent. Then some more went to cover a prescription she'd had to get for a bladder infection the month before, and some other bills that had piled up. Together, they decided to squirrel the rest away, in case something came up over the next couple months. But first, they'd do a little celebrating.

Whenever they felt like good things were on the way, they'd celebrate by drinking some decent whisky, doing a gram of coke, then hitting Snappers, their favourite bar. He'd get the blow from Scotty, an old buddy from high school, and she'd pick out the whisky.

She had Wednesday off this week, so they decided to hit Snappers Tuesday, which also happened to be cheap shooter night. When her shift was finished Tuesday, they had their beer, and each had their own smoke instead of sharing. Then they broke out the Johnny Walker. After they finished half the bottle, they started doing lines and getting ready to go out. By nine, the bottle was empty, so they called a cab and finished most of the coke while they were waiting, leaving just enough for a bump or two when they got home.

Snappers was packed, but they got in because the bouncer was an old buddy of her brother's, and they hit the shooter bar straight away. They each had a shot of tequila and then started dancing. They danced and drank and danced and drank and somewhere along the way they ran into some old friends and they all started drinking together. They laughed and talked and drank and cursed the forces they felt were aligned against them all: the government, rich bastards, the cops. Eddie, who'd been a year behind them in school, was also out of work and off EI. They talked of ways in which they could make some quick money, though nothing would ever come of it in the end.

As the night wore on, they kept drinking and dancing and laughing and scheming, and as last call approached, they were both far gone. She could not stop laughing, and he was having trouble keeping them both upright. When they heard the bell, they rushed to the shooter bar and had one more tequila for the road. Right away, she felt sick, and so she headed for the john. On the way, she bumped into a guy in a Fox Racing jacket, spilling his drink.

"Watch it, bitch," Fox Racing said. His buddies all laughed.

She didn't hear what Fox Racing had said, but he did.

"What the fuck did you just say?"

"I told your woman there to watch it. Spilled my drink. Wanna buy me another?"

"No," he told him. "I don't."

"Then fuck right off," Fox Racing said, and his buddies all laughed again.

"I'm lookin for an apology, pal," he told Fox Racing, whose buddies laughed all the louder. They were all drunk and feeling the way young men feel when they're drunk and together.

"I'll give you an apology," Fox Racing told him, shoving him into a table. Fox Racing was the bigger man by far. After knocking the table over, he fell to the floor. As he was getting up, a work boot cracked into his ribs. He rolled over. He pushed himself up off the floor, then grabbed a bottle off the nearest table and hit Fox Racing in the face. The bottle did not break, but Fox Racing started bleeding anyway, so he kept at him. She came back screaming from the washroom just as Fox Racing got a few shots in. Soon they were both on the floor, rolling and punching. One of Fox Racing's buddies got another kick in as the bouncers broke through the crowd that had gathered around the fight. The lot of them were thrown outside into the bitter cold of early morning, bouncers standing between the two groups, yelling at them to get the fuck out before the cops showed up.

His face was bloody, his side throbbed. He felt a little like puking. She was crying and raging and swearing to God she would kill those motherfuckers. They walked the six blocks home in the cold.

He cleaned his face up, put a bag of iced peas on his side. After he did the bump he'd been saving for himself, his nose started bleeding again. But the pain let off enough that he could sit back and almost relax. She did her bump and started raging about the fuckers in the bar again. They were probably fuckin' homos, she kept repeating. After a while, she went into the bathroom and got sick. When she was through, she came back and slumped down beside him on the couch. She was pale, paler than usual, and she smelled like puke.

"I love you, baby," she said, her face buried in his blood-stained t-shirt.

"I love you too, sweetheart."

RIGHT ON THE BUTTON

"WELL, I NEVER," Doreen Millsap said to her husband Willard, tossing the Saturday paper down in a huff.

"What's that?" Willard said through a mouthful of scrambled eggs, rye toast crumbs peppering his thick gray mustache.

"Says they got a robot down Morris way knows how to curl."

"How's that?"

"They built a robot," Doreen repeated deliberately, for Willard's benefit. "What knows how to curl. Throws a perfect rock every time, or so they say."

"Well," Willard said, reaching across the kitchen table for the Saturday paper. "I never."

Of course, the curling robot was a hot topic of conversation at the Lake Manawaka Curling Club later that evening. Mort Buchanan didn't think much of it, either, but Mort's wife Sharon said she thought there might be something to it.

"If it can throw a perfect rock *despite* Mort's sweeping, the robot's alright by me," Sharon said to a round of belly laughs in the lounge. The two couples were sitting around a table following another easy win for the Millsap/Buchanan mixed doubles rink. Their opponents, the outmatched Burton/Marvin rink, had drawn up an adjacent table to join them and, as losers, had paid for the first round.

"Well," Doreen said, with a shake of her short-cropped gray head, "I never." She took the development of a curling machine as a personal affront.

Whenever you turned on the evening news, or flipped open the Saturday paper, there was some new device meant to make life easier. From self-driving cars to vacuums that do all the work themselves, everything you ever wanted seemed to Doreen to be available at the press of a button on your dang phone.

"What's next," Doreen wondered aloud at breakfast later that week, "a robot priest?"

"Already got 'em," Willard said, washing down a mouthful of hard-boiled egg with a gulp of coffee. "Germans. Or was it the Japanese? Can't rightly recall. Now that I think on it, coulda been the Koreans?"

Doreen could only harumph.

The Millsap/Buchanan rink curled well that winter, placing first in their Saturday night mixed league at the end of the regular season and edging out a victory at the club bonspiel in March. But when it came time to hang up their brooms for the summer, Doreen's robo-bugaboo wouldn't let her alone to enjoy her gardening in peace.

"Looky here, Doreen," Willard said one morning as she came back in from checking her gladiolas in their backyard greenhouse. "Guess they're taking that curling robot on the road this winter?"

"What are you talking about?" Doreen scowled, setting down her trowel.

"That curling robot," Willard said brightly, setting the paper down. "The one what throws them perfect rocks? They're taking it out on the road this winter. To curling rinks. The scientists, that is. Says here you can challenge the machine? For charity, like."

"Well," Doreen said, snatching the paper from Willard's hands in a huff. In a sidebar alongside the story, she found a list of rinks the robot would be visiting later over the next winter. And there it was, the Lake Manawaka Curling Club, Saturday, February 21. Doreen seethed. "I never."

***

Summer passed. When the ice was in come October 1, Doreen Millsap took to it with a steely focus and an intensity that was not lost on her teammates.

"Say, Doreen..." Sharon Buchanan ventured over a round following their first match of the season. "Everything okay?"

"Of course," Doreen replied icily. "Why do you ask?"

"You just seemed a little...*tense* out there."

"I don't know what you're talking about," Doreen huffed. "Just trying to earn the win. Which, of course, *we didn't.*"

Willard raised his eyebrows and looked down into his pint as he took a long, deep drink.

"It's that gosh darn robot ain't it, dear?" he demanded after they'd returned home from the curling rink.

"Dang it, Willard," snapped Doreen, who'd been brusque at best with her teammates and downright rude to Willard all evening. "Why on earth would I let a doggone robot get in my head like that?"

But the next morning, Doreen came clean.

"You're right, hun," she said with a sigh. "I just can't abide the thought of some *egghead* taking the life out of curling like this. I cannot. And I will not. We're taking that danged machine on come February 21. We're gonna put that robot in its gosh darn place!"

"Alright then," Willard said. "Whatever you say, dear."

The next week at the rink, Doreen was no less intense on the ice. But before they took on their opponents for the week, Doreen had taken the time to explain to Mort and Sharon that she was gunning for the chance to out-curl the curling robot. The Buchanans, bless 'em, were on board.

"Why didn't ya say so earlier, Doreen?" Sharon kidded her over drinks after they walloped the Burton/Marvin rink yet again. Having the bugaboo out in the open allowed Doreen to relax, throwing her best, most focused game in some time. "We're always up for a challenge, eh Mort?"

"You bet," Mort added. "Be pretty neat to say we got the best of a robot, wouldn't it?"

"Darn tootin it would," Willard laughed as Doreen blushed into her beer. "And goldarn it, we will!"

***

That evening, the Millsap/Buchanan rink shut down the lounge at the Lake Manawaka Curling Club. Willard borrowed a pad of legal paper from the ladies behind the bar, and the four of them sat, drafting a game plan as to just how they would take on the robot and win. They identified the weaker points of their game and came up with strategies to improve.

As November passed and December wore on, the foursome began showing up on weeknights to use the ice after the Parkland Regional Collegiate teams had finished their weekly matches. They stayed late, working on particular shots, setting up and working their way through likely, then increasingly unlikely, scenarios again and again.

"Three cheers to us, eh," Mort toasted after besting yet another pair of couples the Saturday just before Christmas. Since their salty season-opening loss, the Millsap/Buchanan rink was undefeated. Lately, the games weren't even close. "We're getting there."

"Maybe we are," Doreen admitted, guardedly. That morning's paper had reported on the curling robot's first pair of outings up in Dauphin and Ste. Rose du Lac, where the local clubs' reigning junior, senior, and master rinks had taken on the robot and its egghead helpers. They'd lost, each of them in turn; the robot undefeated. "But we got a ways to go yet."

As winter passed, Doreen honed her game with precision. Those who'd known her forty years earlier, before the kids, when she'd won a pair of buffaloes as a third and come within a shot as a skip herself a few years later, swore that she was better now than she had ever been then. More consistent, at least. But at home, Willard noticed that the strain was wearing on his wife.

"Bad night again, dear?" he'd ask over breakfast.

"Did I keep you up?" she asked, slumping into a seat at the kitchen table.

"Not really," Willard lied, handing her a cup of coffee.

"Sorry, dear," she said, bags hanging under her tired blue eyes. Like as not, he'd been kept up as Doreen tossed and turned, muttering in her sleep throughout those long winter nights leading up to the showdown. "It's the same dang dream every night. That friggin' robot, red eyes flashing like something outta one of those space movies Bobby used to make us watch, beeping and sputtering its way down the ice. And it keeps throwing perfect rocks, one after another until the dang thing goes berserk and starts chucking 'em all over the dang place, smashing up the ice and ruining everything. It's horrible. I wake up with the cold sweats."

"I know, hon," Willard sighed. "I know."

***

When they met Mort and Sharon at the rink later that afternoon to prepare for the match, the robot's handlers—dressed in matching curling jackets with the university's crest on one shoulder, the Morris Curling Club crest on the other—were setting up shop on the western-most rink.

"How we feeling today?" Sharon asked the Millsaps with a slightly nervous edge to her voice.

"I'm ready," Doreen said, with a determined look in her eye that belied her lack of sleep. "Ready and raring to go."

"That's the spirit, love." Willard smiled broadly. After the kids had been born, curling had become something Doreen and Willard did on the weekend, not something they lived for. But she'd never stopped loving the game. She never abandoned it. It had always been there for her, every winter, year in, year out. With the kids and their jobs and the mortgage and their own ailing parents, the game just didn't seem as important as real life. Something, though, had changed this winter. Doreen had something to prove, to herself if no one else. Willard saw that, and he accepted it. And Doreen loved that in her husband. He was all in, as he always had been. "Let's show 'em what we got, eh?"

A half hour later, the eggheads in their university duds rolled in a heavy-duty road case on a dolly. Doreen and the gang stopped to stare. At the far end of the rink, the handlers popped the clasps holding the case together, removing padded panels delicately before pulling the machine out to the ice.

At rest, the machine looked a little like a glossy black and white vacuum cleaner. As a woman from the team sat, tapping at a laptop, the machine began to move forward, rolling on four large rubber wheels up to the point slightly ahead of the hack. The robot advanced until the rock came to rest within the metal horseshoe-shaped corral at the front of the machine, buffered by a pair of padded whirligigs that, when engaged, spun the rock a clock or counterclockwise.

Then, what Doreen could only assume was the robot's "head" rose up from its body on a telescoping, crane-like neck to scan the ice's surface with a row of blinking red "eyes." When it retracted, the whirligigs set to spinning. The wheels rolled the robot towards the hog line with subtly increasing speed. Delicately, the robot released the rock, sending it spinning down the ice.

"Hoo boy," Mort whistled as the rock came to rest delicately, perfectly on the button.

While Doreen had seen pictures and videos of the robot in action, and had dreamed of some demonic version of the devilish device more times than she cared to admit, seeing her adversary in person had an unexpected calming effect on her. The machine's first perfect, soulless throws only confirmed what she'd long suspected.

"We can beat it," she whispered, tired eyes sparkling. "Danged if we don't."

***

Doreen led the way to where the science types were waiting. Behind the glass, the crowd in the lounge and inside the main floor lobby of the old Lake Manawaka Curling Club had grown considerably. Doreen could feel their eyes on her as she walked up to shake hands with the lead researcher.

"This should be fun," the lead scientist, a man of about their own age, told Doreen and her team. "Good luck."

Doreen felt the weight of the eyes of the crowd on her, but she ignored them.

"Game on," she replied.

The robot rolled slowly onto the ice. A few moments later, it rolled forward again, propelling the yellow-topped rock out of the hack and down the long sheet of ice. The rock, spinning silently, came slowly to rest right on the button.

"Jesus Murphy," Mort whispered as the robot backed itself up the makeshift ramp off the ice. "Right on the money."

"Nevermind," dismissed Doreen with a contemptuous snicker. "We'll show them."

And show them they did. Shot for shot, Doreen and the gang kept knocking the robot's rocks into the backboards. But no matter how their own rocks came to rest, the robot cleared them.

"Like a dang table tennis match," Willard muttered.

When the end was over, both teams left a rock in play. With the blank end, the robot kept the hammer and they went at it again. Doreen worked to keep the game tight, calling rocks into positions she knew would give her opponent the least advantage possible. At the end of the third, the robot's team scored, tying the game.

After a blank fourth end, the robot's rink came up with two points in the fifth to go up 3-2. The interns and scientists pumped their fists, exchanging high fives.

"Dang ice is getting keen," Mort cussed unconvincingly after they were unable to convert with the hammer in the sixth end, which ended in another blank.

From there, though, things began to fall apart.

In the ninth end, Doreen and the gang inadvertently scored one to tie after being unable to clear the house with the final rock, giving the robot back the hammer for the final end.

"Dog gone it," Doreen cursed as the two rinks huddled together before the tenth and potentially final end. "Stupid, stupid, stupid."

Sharon and Mort exchanged nervous glances, while Willard puffed out his cheeks before letting out a slow breath. He hadn't seen his wife so worked up in years.

"Let's just take 'er easy here and do the best we can," he said, laying a soft hand on Doreen's shoulder. "We done pretty darn decent, so far."

"Alright," Doreen said, setting her jaw with a curt nod of her head before heading to the far end of the rink. The eyes in the crowd took it all in, nervously. "You're right. Let's do this."

Under Doreen's direction, Mort threw a high guard just inside the house. The robot countered cooly with a low guard inside. Mort's next shot was to take the robot's rock out. But it didn't come with enough jam to fully clear, instead settling low in the house next to the yellow. With a whirr, the robot slid one right past the high guard, banging both the low yellow and red rocks out of play. With her first rock, Sharon took the opposition out. In response, the robot threaded its next rock past the high red guard to rest right on the button.

"Give 'em hell, hon," Willard whispered, squeezing Doreen's elbow as they passed on the ice, Willard to take up the skip spot and Doreen headed to the hack. "You got this."

Doreen settled herself down to the ice, left foot nestled comfortably in the hack. She looked up at Willard standing down the ice, broom indicating the spot just above and to the right of the yellow rocks where she should aim, his right arm indicating the curl. She nodded.

Willard, God bless him, knew Doreen's mind nearly as well as she did, after all the years they'd spent together. She wrapped the fingers of her right hand around the handle of her last rock. With her left hand, she gripped her broom. She took a deep breath, steadied herself, and curled.

"Easy now, easy," Doreen began instructing her rock before she'd even finished sliding down the ice towards the hog line. Immediately, she knew she'd sent it down the sheet with too much force, considering how keen the ice had become. At least, she told herself, she hadn't turned out too hard.

"Right off," Doreen called to Mort and Sharon as they moved into the position. "No! Never, never!"

The red rock spun counterclockwise as it hurled down towards the house, edging ever so slowly across to the left. It was close. But it was not enough. Sharon and Mort abandoned their charge as the red rock barreled by its own high guard, past the yellow rock closest to the button before crashing into the hindmost yellow rock, sending it careening out of play.

"Well," Doreen sighed. Her shoulders slumped as the red rock itself spun uselessly to the right sideboard, leaving the yellow rocks in the house untouched. Willard, Sharon, and Mort looked on, aghast, as the eggheads high-fived around them and the robot stood, whirring and beeping to itself, oblivious. "I never."

"We tried, love," he told her, later that evening for what must have been the tenth time that evening. "We done our best. You skipped a heck of a game, Dor. A heck of a game. Really."

"I know," Doreen replied, forcing a ghost of a smile to wash over her face. Ahead, the brake lights of a truck blinked through the February darkness like the eyes of the robot. "I know, dear."

THE CHASM

THE CHASM IS GROWING.

That's what the old man on the line told me. I looked at the phone like you gotta be fucking kidding me. The calls we get sometimes.

Which chasm is that, sir? I was trying to sound diplomatic. Specifically.

The big one, the old man said. I could tell he was old because his voice sounded the way a rotten shed looks when it's slowly returning to earth. It's getting bigger.

One moment, sir. I opened a new file on the computer. Let me just make sure I get all the details down here.

Working for the government, it's not all dog fucking and union breaks. There's some real wackadoodle crap we've got to wade through in order to put the minds of taxpayers at ease every now and again.

Walter, the old man, explained that the chasm out back of the seniors complex had been there for years. You know the one, he repeated. Nobody had fallen in that he knew of, but it was only a matter of time. Mark my words young lady, he repeated. Nothing good can come of this.

I understand, I assured him. Someone would be by soon to examine the chasm.

But soon wasn't good enough for Walter.

No time to muck about, he maintained. The chasm, it's growing.

I'll get someone right on it, I told him. I hung up, sending the report wherever it went when you clicked Send. Figured, that's the end of that.

Wrong.

Next day, middle-manager waddles over to my desk first thing. Hadn't even had two sips of my coffee yet.

You take the call on the chasm? Don't know why he asked. He knows I did. Everything we do is logged. Sure, I shrug. Middle-manager sighs. He waves for me to follow as he waddles off, leading me to a room full of high vis protective gear, tells me to find a vest, gloves, and safety glasses that fit. Tells me *I'm* going to check out this chasm.

Usually, there's a crew that would handle that sort of stuff. Trees that have fallen over the road, bigfoot sightings, water main breaks. That kinda crap. In two years in this department, I've never once been sent out to follow up on the calls we get, crank or otherwise. Why me?

Middle-manager shrugs. Orders from above. Or someone's on vacation, stress leave, whatever. I dig through the stacks and find the smallest safety vest and gloves they've got (still too big) and a pair of plastic safety glasses. Middle-manager tosses me a set of keys, metal fob with 462 stamped on it.

Truck's in the garage, he grunts. Send a report up soon as you're back. Take some pictures with your phone. You know the drill.

I don't. Not really. But he's already waddling off. Well. How hard can it be?

Half-hour later I pull up to Walter's old folks home in a big old GMC with government plates and peeling decals on the side. Number 462. It's fun driving the big old beast around town. Usually, I take the bus. I'm starting to think my license expired some time back, but I'm not even certain I have it on me. Oh well. Middle-manager should have confirmed before he flipped me the keys.

At the old folks home, I pull up to the curb, get the four-ways flashing, and wander into reception where I tell the guy behind the counter I'm here to inspect the chasm.

Right this way, reception guy says. Please.

We make our way down a long corridor, reception guy unlocking each set of closed double doors with a keycard attached to his belt by a retractable zip line. Each time, the thing whirrs this high-pitched whirr that reminds me of the dentist. Reception guy doesn't seem to notice. Maybe he likes it?

Before long we're out back.

Here it is, reception guy says. I whistle. No kidding. We're standing on the edge of a chasm alright.

Reception guy, he stands next to me, hands on his hips. I pull out my work phone, take a few photos. But it's hard to really get a good sense of perspective this close. It just looks empty.

Any chance we can get up to the roof?

Reception guy frowns. Let me make a couple calls, he says, pulling out a phone. I leave him to mumble my request up the ladder and lean into the chasm for a closer look. It's deep and dark with no discernible bottom. Across, it's a good twenty feet, easy. Maybe twice as long. No safety signage in sight. Walter's right: It's a miracle nobody has fallen in yet.

How long's this been here? I ask. Reception guy just holds up a finger, nodding along to whatever's being said on the other end of his phone. He tucks it back into his pocket. Follow me.

I ask him again, as we climb the stairs up to the roof. But it's no use.

Couldn't tell you, reception guy wheezes. I'm new here.

We step out onto the roof and sure enough, from the edge, I can take a decent photo of the chasm, though it just looks like a big black empty blob or a gross fat leech, against the yellowing grass of the lawn that surrounds it. I snap a couple pics anyhow. Nice view, I offer. Reception guy nods, squinting against the glare of the late morning sun. We head back down.

On the ground, reception guy heads off to track someone down who can tell me something, anything, while I crouch down on the lip of the chasm, peering into the depth.

It's hard to say just what I saw down there. Nothing, really. The chasm is deep and it is dark and it seems to go on forever and I told you that already.

Sound echoed down off the dirt walls but at some point seemed to just disappear or taper off. No sound seemed to emanate upwards, exactly, though I could be wrong. There was something, a hum or vibration maybe, which I found highly unsettling. Maybe it was nothing. Maybe I imagined it. But sitting there, staring down, I felt the dread that I'd heard in Walter's voice over the phone. Made me want to puke. You know how when you listen to a conch shell, you know that's not the sea you hear. But if it's not the sea, then what is it?

Don't ask me. I just work here.

Finally, reception guy returned with a power suit lady in tow. He introduced her as the facility manager, though I didn't catch her name. Probably should have asked, but here we are. Instead I say, How long has this thing been here anyway?

Some time now, the facility manager replies, bored. Years. But it wasn't always so large. I'm not sure what you can do about it, though. This isn't the first time someone's come out to take a look at it.

I can see how that would be concerning. Why hadn't middle-manager told me this was an ongoing issue? Maybe he didn't know. He doesn't seem to know much of anything, really. A lot of reports go flying through the office. After a while, they kind of all blur together. Even something this big could get lost, in time.

We've grown used to it, facility manager tells me. Most of us, anyway.

I guess, I say.

Can't seem to fill it in, the facility manager says. Lord knows we tried. We've completely blown our budget on safety fencing. But it just keeps falling in. No getting that money back.

When I get back to the office, I give the middle-manager back the keys to the truck and file my report, pics and all. I haven't heard anything about the chasm since. Not from middle- or upper-management. Not from Walter, the receptionist, or the facility manager at the old folks home either. Nada.

Yet, it still bothers me. Where did the big hole come from, anyway? Where does it lead to? It has to end somewhere, right? How many more are out there? How long till Walter and the rest of the old fogies housed in that old building are swallowed whole?

I tried searching through our system, at work, for some answers. Zip-zilch-zero. Our system doesn't work that way. It's one way. Info goes in and it flows to where it needs to flow. Generally, that works out just fine. Generally, who cares, right?

When I leave the office at five each day, I have a strict, no exceptions policy of shutting my work brain off completely.

But I can't quite pull that off anymore.

THE JACKALOPE

When Tony first spotted the jackalope, he nearly choked on his pastrami on rye.

He'd been eating his lunch on the loading dock of the mattress factory where he worked. Once he'd cleared his windpipe and caught his breath, Tony hopped down and took a step towards the chain-link fence that separated the mattress factory from the grassy knoll in front of the neighbouring potato chip plant. He blinked his eyes, squinted against the glare of the sun. The rabbit-thing was still there, soaking up the sun, crisp April breeze ruffling its ruddy-brown fur.

"Holy smokes," Tony gasped, wishing his buddy Javier had joined him for lunch so they could confirm what his eyes were seeing. "That's a goddamn jackalope!"

Indeed it was. Or at least, that's what it appeared to be. When Tony moved to get a closer look, the animal bolted, disappearing in the underbrush along the rail spur that serviced the back lots.

A devotee of *Red Dead Redemption* since way back, Tony was familiar with jackalopes. He'd never seen one though. He'd never even been sure if they were real or not—he'd never paid much attention to science, or anything really, in school— until that day on the loading dock. But when he tried to tell his buddies at the bar after work about it, they all laughed at him.

"That's a fairy tale, dummy," Jimbo said, voice heavy with drink and derision. "You stupid or something? Ain't no such thing."

"But I seen it," Tony implored, heart sinking. "Seriously."

"Ya right," Jimbo laughed. "And I fucked a mermaid out in Lake Manawaka last summer. Ha!"

Javier, who worked next to Tony on the factory floor, was more diplomatic.

"I do not believe you," Javier told him, shaking his head slowly. "Such a creature would be an abomination unto God."

Still Javier, who was Tony's only semblance of a pal outside of his bar buddies, agreed to eat his lunch on the loading dock with him the next day. When their thirty minutes were up, though, and they'd seen neither hide nor hair of the jackalope, Javier shook his head again, eyebrows raised dubiously. After that, Tony went back to eating his lunch alone, eyes scanning the knoll across the way as it grew greener by the day.

It wasn't until the Friday before the May long weekend that the jackalope made another appearance. Even then, Tony almost missed it. He'd finished his corned beef, was in the process of crumpling up the wax paper wrap and hopping to his feet to dust the crumbs off his lap, when out of the corner of his eye he caught a downy blur. Tony froze.

There it was, flaring its nostrils against the breeze on the far side of the spur line.

Slowly, Tony reached out for his phone. Slower still, he brought it up, pointed the lens towards the jackalope. Carefully, Tony spread his fingers across the screen to zoom in. Then, he pressed the red button rapidly once, twice, three times, four.

But Tony hadn't muted his phone. The rapid clicking sound representing the digital shutter spooked his subject and it bolted back again from whence it came.

"Shoot," Tony fumed. But he took solace in the fact that his shutter had indeed clicked, that he'd captured the jackalope, digitally at least. He flipped through the photos he'd captured. A tad out of focus, he had to admit, but good enough, Tony figured.

"This is just a big rabbit, no?" Javier said after giving the pics a look. "Diseased, maybe?"

After that, Tony didn't show the photos to any of his other buddies. He didn't even bother stopping by the bar after work, heading straight home instead. Tony knew they'd just laugh at him. All those guys did was laugh at him like he was only some kind of hayseed moron, just because he didn't know about animals, or sports or taxes or girls or any of the other crap they went on and on about every night while they tipped their Bud heavies back. Sure, Tony hadn't done much with life, before or after moving to the city a few years out of high school. He may not be wise to the ways of the world, but dang it, Tony had found himself something rare, something he could call his own.

On his drive home, Tony hatched a plan. Those ding dongs wouldn't be laughing if he caught the thing, would they? He'd probably make it on the local news and everything.

Saturday morning, Tony made a call and arranged to rent a cat trap from the humane society. He paid the rental fee and the deposit in cash then drove across town to the industrial park.

Tony stopped at a liquor store and bought a bottle of Five Star rye whisky on the way. He'd read online during one of many Reddit deep dives that the animals fancied firewater, of all things. And while most of what he'd read online on the subject of the jackalope had seemed incredible at best, Tony didn't have much else to go on. So Five Star rye whisky it was.

Tony parked in his usual spot behind the mattress factory. He tucked the bottle of rye into a sack and, with the sun just beginning to climb high into the mid-morning sky, grabbed the trap and started out.

Tony nestled the trap down into the brush between two scraggly willows a ways west down the rail line and pulled the whisky from his bag. Then he unscrewed the cap and poured an ounce into an empty sour cream container he'd brought from home.

Carefully, he placed the container deep within the trap, then shuffled back to his car.

But the trap remained empty all morning. As the shadows stretched out to the east, Tony remained, slouched behind the wheel, staring down the line. Apart from a dirty old crow that'd poked around for a while, Tony hadn't seen another living thing all day.

The industrial park was bathed in twilight when he got up to approach the trap, just to check it out. He broke into a jog as he noticed its door was closed.

"Oh boy," Tony whistled, flashlight banging around in his backpack along with the bottle of whisky as he raced along the tracks. "Oh boy, oh boy."

Sure enough, the trap had been sprung, the door locked tight. In the mounting gloom, Tony couldn't see inside beyond the metal grate. He crouched down, panting, gravel crunching under his boots. Tony cleared his throat, at a loss as to what to say or do.

"Hello?" he stammered. "You in there, little buddy?"

The trap lay still beneath the lanky willows. Heart pounding, Tony couldn't tell if he'd heard something from the back of the plastic box, or if it were only the wind. He pulled the flashlight out of the sack, clicked the beam on.

He took a deep breath, leaned in, and flashed the light at the back of the trap.

Empty.

The trap had been sprung, the gate shut and locked, but the cage itself was vacant, save for the sour cream container he'd used for bait. But, unclasping the gate for a closer look, Tony noticed that the sour cream container had been drained.

"What the heck?"

Hair rising on his neck, Tony shut off the flashlight, turned to look up at the few stars he could see above the dull glow of the industrial park. Although he was most certainly alone, Tony had the distinct feeling of being watched when he knelt in the gravel to reset the trap. He sloshed a liberal amount of whisky into the plastic cup before taking a long pull himself and retreating to the front seat of his car.

Tony stared into the gloom for over an hour, hoping to catch a glimpse of something in the darkness, though he saw no discernible movement of any kind. Yet, when he ventured out to check the trap, once again he found it snapped shut, whisky gone.

"Hot dang," he cursed, scrambling to his feet and bolting back towards his car as fear rippled through him. "Something's up."

He tossed his sack into the back seat, locked the doors, and fumbled for his keys, certain that somebody was watching him. That somebody was playing a dirty trick on him. He cranked the engine and sped off towards his apartment.

Bright and early the next morning, far from rested, Tony was back at the industrial park.

He'd lain awake throughout the night, working the situation over and over again. The only people, he figured, who would go to any length to pull a prank on him were Jimbo and the boys from the bar. And there was no way that they had known he'd been down behind the mattress factory all day. The only other possibility, remote as it was, was Javier. But a prankster Javier was not. Besides, Javier had proudly told

Tony that he was taking his family out camping for the long weekend, at least a hundred miles from the scene.

Tony was certain it was none other than the jackalope itself that had taken his whisky and sprung his trap. The beast, it stood to reason, was playing him for a fool.

Frankly, Tony had had enough of being played for a fool. He told himself as much as he sped across town Sunday morning, pumping himself up for a long day, perhaps even a long night waiting for the jackalope to show its ruddy, mottled coat. Tony swore that he would not leave without catching the animal. He would show the boys at the bar, Javier, his parents back home, that he had found something, something special. He would show them all, he swore. Then, he took a swig from his bottle to fortify himself to the task at hand.

Tony set the trap further down the line this time. He dispensed with the sour cream container, pouring the whisky instead in a shallow puddle on the floor of the trap itself, though his reasons for doing so were unclear. Perhaps, he thought, the beast would go wild trying to lick the booze up and stumble into captivity.

Then, he doubled back and took a position behind a stack of pallets downwind of the trap. Changing things up, he figured, could work in his favor. It couldn't hurt, anyway.

Growing frustrated and bored as the hours passed with no sign of the jackalope, nor of any prankster, human or otherwise, Tony started nipping frequently from the bottle of rye.

In the sixth hour, when Tony got up to take a leak, he caught a glimpse of something moving from the corner of his eye. His head snapped back in the direction of the trap and there it was.

"Oh baby," Tony whispered, barely noticing the hot piss splashing his leg, focused as he was on the animal sniffing cautiously at the entrance to the trap. "Oh baby!"

The beast froze, stately little antlers poking up at the blue sky above, ears twitching in Tony's direction, before shifting its gaze to scan both sides of the train tracks. Tony froze too, his heart hammering blood through his ears as his prey turned tail and retreated cautiously into the bushes. Tony had trouble tracking its dunny coat through the scrub, but he thought he could see where it had come to rest up. Staring, he shifted himself into a crouch, and settled in to wait the beast out.

Hours later, sun sinking in the west, the jackalope finally re-emerged. Tony, legs and back aching from crouching, his stomach grumbling, tensed. His eyes widened, dry lips twisted into a grin as the jackalope crept out from the shadows and made its way cautiously towards the trap.

"Come on," Tony whispered into the wind. "Come on now."

Tony could see it all play out before him. Vindicated, his cunning and commitment to the truth would be celebrated far and wide. No more would his dullard buddies mock him, but rather they would hold him up as something of a hero per-haps, or, at the very least, someone worthy of respect and def-erence to all things trap- or beast-related. His parents would brag to anyone back in Lake Manawaka whose ear they could bend, their son a hero, a minor celebrity at least.

But the jackalope just stood there, its head near the en-trance to the trap, tail facing Tony, tongue lapping up the am-ber liquid within.

"Internet didn't lie," he muttered, stunned. "Dang thing's drinking the whisky."

Tony watched as the jackalope drank up the puddle before it, waiting for the thirsty beast to reach into the trap just a step too far. But that moment never came. Instead, it stepped back out and raised its antlers and ears to the wind, before wander-ing off down the tracks from whence it had first come.

Tony walked calmly down the tracks after it. When he got to the trap, he unscrewed the cap to the whisky bottle and made a show of tossing it away into the bush. He poured another generous splash of rye into the trap before retreating slowly to his car, then doubling back to crouch behind the blind again, sipping whisky.

As the sun set, and boredom settled in with the chill of darkness, Tony found that the booze had crept up on him. Before long, Tony was drunk. He certainly hadn't meant for it to happen. But there he was, crouched in the bushes by the spur line muttering to himself, drunk.

A little after midnight, Tony caught a flash of something moving in the darkness. Drunk as he was, Tony snapped back into focus. Silent, still, he peered across the distance at the shadow moving towards the trap. Though he couldn't see much, he felt certain that it was the jackalope and that, finally, the time had come.

"Here we go," Tony whispered excitedly. "Here we go."

Bottle in hand, Tony lurched abruptly out from behind the pallet blind in the direction of the trap. Stumbling, gravel crunching loudly beneath his sneakers, he made his mad dash towards the open trap.

Later, when he'd reflect back on that evening, Tony would often wonder what would have happened if he hadn't bolted, half blind with drink, down the spur line at that moment. Would the jackalope have tripped the trap on his own, if given enough time? Would he have found an opportunity to surprise the beast later on, from a better vantage point, with some measure of success? Or, at the very least, could he have saved himself some measure of pain and shame?

Sprinting sloppily, Tony kept his eyes on the jackalope, which stood with a tentative front paw in the air just outside of the trap's door.

"Come on," Tony wheezed, gaining uneven ground. "Don't go."

The jackalope crouched back, pressing its soft underbelly to the cold ground, flattening its ears along its back, tiny antlers raised defiantly. Tony came at it, full on, arms spread wide. A low growl rose from his belly, rising to a roar as he gained the top of the rail bed. The jackalope tensed, frozen in place as Tony's roar turned to a startled scream when his foot caught the rail line and he was sent sprawling through the air towards the beast.

The last thing Tony saw before he hit the rail bed were the jackalope's eyes, which looked red in the gloom, staring deep into his own. Mocking him. Tony knew then that the thing had been playing him all along. Playing him for a goddamn fool. Then he hit the ground, headfirst into the solid steel rail line.

When he came to, hours later, soaked in dew in the early morning gloom, a security guard was shaking him awake with the toe of her boot. Tony blinked. The empty whisky bottle lay not far from the empty trap. Tony moaned as awareness and pain flooded back to him from the void.

"What the heck you doin' here, bud?" the security guard asked as Tony pushed himself gingerly up off the ground to his knees. "You been drinkin?"

"No," Tony croaked. Everything hurt. He raised a hand, felt the scabby goose egg swelling from his skull. He reeked of stale whisky and piss, the inside of his mouth tasted like a sewer grate. "Well, a little, maybe. I . . . It's a long story."

Unimpressed, the security guard shook her head sternly.

"This here's private property," she told Tony, drawing herself up a little taller. "You should go home. Have a shower. Sleep it off."

Dejected, hungover, Tony could only nod his head meekly as he gathered the cat trap and the empty bottle. The guard followed him to his car. As Tony opened the door, he paused to glance back up the rail line.

Over the shoulder of the security guard, not far from where he'd lain, the jackalope sat hunched in the bushes. Staring at him.

Eyes wide, Tony stopped short. His mouth fell open.

"Forget something, bud?" the security guard asked impatiently.

The jackalope held his gaze, daring him to action. But there was no way Tony could get past her—in his current state, or otherwise—and even then, he had little hope of catching up to the jackalope, did he?

Tony blinked again, rubbed his bloody face vigorously. When he opened his eyes, the jackalope was gone.

"No," Tony said, his voice a dry, empty croak in the light morning breeze. In the back of his mind, he heard the boys at the bar just a howling. "Nothing at all."

TOO CRUNCHY

AFTER YEARS OF PUSHING PENCILS hard, one day Gary got the big promotion at the chip factory.

Finally, he told himself, his wife, anyone who'd listen, he'd be the one calling the shots.

Gary loved the flavours the chip factory pumped out. Sour-Cream-N'-Onion-O-Rama. Bold Bacon Explosion. Barbecue Massacre. A big fan from way back, Gary couldn't get enough.

What bugged him about the chips was the crunch.

Love the taste, he'd tell his wife, his coworkers, anyone who'd listen. Neighbours, cashiers, the clergy. Whoever. But they're just too crunchy!

After the promotion, everyone started listening. Started showing some respect. The boys all bought him drinks at the bar. His wife started blowing him again. Even the neighbourhood dogs stopped shitting on Gary's lawn. It was like magic.

With Gary calling the shots, it wasn't long before the chip factory cut back on the crunch. And how.

A big fan, Gary, of the new not crunchy chips. All the great taste, he'd say as he stuffed his mouth, without that hard crunch. I could eat these all day!

Some days, he did. Gary couldn't get enough of the new limp chips. So tasty, so not crunchy. So not painful when he mashed them up with his soft, weak teeth. He'd lick his dry lips with his pasty pale tongue and shove another handful down the hatch, his long fingers dusted with fiery fiesta flavour flakes.

Things were just tickety-boo for old Gary.

But not everyone was a fan of the limp chips. No sir. They still craved the flavours alright. The chips themselves, though? Not so much.

Too soft, his wife, coworkers, everyone agreed. Why mess with success?

The chip factory bean counters agreed. Nobody wanted the mushy chips. They bought other kinds instead. Hard kinds, crunchy kinds. Chip factory execs would abide by the changes no more.

Gary, he lost his job. He was out on his ass. Pow! Sure enough, none of the boys from the factory would go out for drinks with him anymore. His wife stopped blowing him, demanding he start playing the crypto markets between filling out new job applications. Dog turds repopulated his once pristine lawn. Poor Gary.

The chips? They got crunchy again in a hurry. So, so crunchy. Crunchier, even, than before.

Even though he had to patiently allow the chips to soften in his soggy little mouth before he took each bite, not unlike a feeble child, Gary still loved those flavours like brothers.

DAD'S DAY AT THE LOCAL ZOO

IT WAS FATHER'S DAY, which is why the kids and I went to the zoo to begin with.

We used to take the kids to the zoo, back when they were little and me and their mom were still together. Even though it was one of their favourite spots, it kinda made me sad. All those majestic beasts locked up, their wild spirits broken like the rest of us. But good days can be hard to come by. If it made the kids happy, I made myself see past it.

Once, when a whole group of us were in the monkey house together, I bet some other dad twenty bucks that if this one old chimp scratched his ass, he'd sniff his finger straight away. Seemed like a sure bet to me. If those crude fuckers aren't jerking off for all to see they're flinging their turds at each other. But I lost. Chimp just sat there, picking his ear. When I paid up, I realized I didn't have any more cash left for the ice-cream stand, and the credit cards were already maxed. Kids cried the whole way home. Ex wouldn't let me hear the end of it for weeks. As if I could just ask for my twenty bucks back. As if any other day of the week, that bet doesn't pay off.

Bengal tiger, he's a real hit with the kids. Even now. You can hear him roar across the entire park. If that old bastard is storming back and forth along the perimeter of his enclosure, a crowd gathers every time. Once, he pissed a stream right through the fence so hard some kid got soaked from head to toe.

Good luck, I'm told, getting tiger piss on you. Would have been nice if a little had splashed over our way. Could have used a little luck, these past couple years. But here we are, another day older, insurmountably in debt.

Ex-wife and I, we've been divorced now two years, going on forever it feels like. She'd tell you it was all my fault. She's not wrong. Not entirely. But we'd be drifting apart for years. Things change, people change. Marriage is not a zoo. At least, it shouldn't be.

The kids, they don't enjoy it as much, now that they're older. The zoo, that is. But I don't know what else to do with them when we get a weekend together. Which is rare enough, seeing as their mother's got full custody and all. Movies are too goddamn expensive nowadays and don't even get me started on museums. Their mother says I can't take them to the track or a ball game or mini-golf or anywhere I might place a wager anymore under any circumstances. So, off we go to the zoo, under oath not to engage in side-bets on animal behaviour. Again.

Maybe, in a way, I'm hoping for a little of the old magic. The easy awe. Like a couple hours with the animals could undo all the hurt that's piled up over the years. Like an ice cream cone and something from the gift shop—a tiger, a wolf, or an eagle shirt, maybe—can mend broken promises. A dad's gotta try, right? Even when neither of my kids get me so much as a Father's Day card. I guess I can't say I blame 'em. But still, it stings.

My oldest, she's rolling her eyes from the moment we pull into the parking lot, dragging the heels of her expensive sneakers as we approach the front gate. As the turnstiles flap behind us, she goes, Ever wonder what would happen if the animals got out, dad?

What if, eh?

That's the thrill of the place, at heart. The majesty of nature, stuck locked in a goddamn cage. But they're still wild, deep in their souls. Aren't they?

Aren't we all?

My cousin Larry, he worked at a zoo. Not this one. One out west. Same thing, basically though, with the cages and the locks, right? He told me once when we were drinking that there's a way to short circuit the alarm system in any of these places. Something to do with the way they're wired together and looping the five-second delay.

After that, he said, anyone can let the animals loose. Just a matter of opening the fuckin doors, bro. Said it like it happened all the time. Or could happen at any time, if you knew what Larry knew. I didn't believe him, then.

But when the girl, already bored out of her mind and we ain't even through the gates yet, goes, What if the animals get out? I remembered Larry's story and it made me wonder. So I go, Let's find out, sweetheart.

The girl, she just gives me the look, like I was born a moron. You got kids, you'll know the one. Like every mistake we ever made was on purpose. Like we're not out there every day trying our best to provide for 'em, to make a better life for 'em. Like we shoulda known those bets we made that didn't pay off weren't ever gonna and done something different from Day 1.

Me, I just chuckle. When you got nothing, you got nothing to lose. George Thorogood say that? If he didn't, he shoulda.

Anyhow, now I'm on the hunt, see. Just waiting to come across one of those golf carts the parkies leave unattended now and then. Doesn't take long, either. There's one outside a shitter, next to the snowy owls and the elk. Keys are in the ignition.

What are you doing, dad? my boy asks, eyes wide behind his glasses as I walk over and help myself. He's got a nervous look, but like he's excited too. Always been a bit of a risk-taker, the boy. Reminds me of me, the scamp. Those aren't your keys.

I go, You wanna know what happens if the animals get out or what?

The kids, they look at each other. But when they look back at me, they're not looking at me like I was born stupid no more. No sir. They got the look like they used to, back when they were just little and thought I could do no wrong. Before I lost the house and all our money and the wife took 'em both and moved in with her sister, leaving me high and dry.

Let's just see what happens, I tell the kids as I walk casually over to the door of the owls' cage. The kids fall in line, giggling into their hands. They got that look again like when I'd come home from work back in the day and it was time to have some fun. Like I got all the answers. I grin back, hoping to hell Larry was telling the truth for once.

See, Larry'd been a liar ever since we were kids. He'd say his dad could hit a baseball so hard it would bust those seams right open and the insides would unwind so you'd never see them again. Or how he could pop a wheelie on his dirt bike and ride it out a quarter mile, no problem. Born bullshitter, Larry.

But he wasn't bullshitting about this trick with the keys and zoo's alarm system. No siree.

Larry's jimmy-rig move on the locks worked. Easy peasy, lemon squeezy.

Just like that, we're setting the animals free.

Those snowy owls, boy, they went like greased lightning once that cage door swung open. Bye-bye, birdies! The elk didn't seem to have a clue that freedom lay just a hop, skip, and a jump over the moat, but maybe they figured it out in time. We never stuck around to find out. For all I know, they're headed north right now, making for the tundra.

After that, we opened every door we came across, snaking our way through the zoo like we owned the place. The kids were loving it. I mean, they were eating it up, skipping ahead, tugging at my hand just like they did in the old days—going, Come on daddy, come on!—eager as beavers to free the next group of beasts.

Let me tell ya, it was something, watching all those colourful birds take to the skies one-by-one. The toucan and cockatoo, flying south as fast as the wind and their wings could take them. Seeing that big bastard Steller's sea eagle flap those gigantic wings and just take off had what's left of my hair standing on end.

Whoa, the boy said, grabbing my hand for the first time in months, years even. Look at the size of that thing!

You don't see that every day, I told my son, holding his little fingers tight, but not too tight. Sure as hell no.

We all smiled wide to see the antelope, the emu, and the ibex make their breaks for it. We even went into the monkey house to let the chimps and the apes loose. It was something, seeing those gibbons scoop their little ones up onto their backs before swinging out the cage doors to freedom.

Aww, my daughter cooed, leaning in for an all-too-rare hug. They're sooooo cute!

They sure are, I agreed. Though my heart was fit to burst, with the kids so close for the first time in ages, I was also filled with sadness. I wished, for about the millionth time, that I hadn't fucked everything up the way I had, going for broke again and again and always falling short. It wasn't that I didn't love my kids as much as the gibbon carrying its young on its back up and out of those cages to freedom and a life in the wild. It's that I wasn't able to, when the chips were down. They sure are, sweetheart.

Now, I'll admit that things got a little dicey when we got to the big cats.

Never turn your back on these suckers, I kept repeating in a low voice as we backed away from the newly freed mountain lions. Believe you me, I told 'em, you give a cougar an inch, she'll take a mile.

Don't get me wrong. I was always between the kids and the kitties. They were never in any real danger. Nothing I couldn't handle. Not that it mattered, in the end. Maybe those felines knew we'd freed 'em. Or maybe we just didn't smell appetizing. Whatever it was, they never bothered us. Not one of 'em. Not once. Not even that mean old Bengal. He just sniffed, then turned and tore off the other way.

Course, once the other patrons caught wind of what was happening, all hell broke loose. I mean it was bananas, like the floor at a Destroyers concert where everyone's been day drinking. But the kids, they were eating it up. I never seen 'em laugh so much, not since they were knee-high to a grasshopper and a visit from the tickle-monster was the funniest thing they could ever imagine. Back when their love for me knew no bounds.

We made it as far as the gates, laughing and holding hands and just having the best of times, when this old timer in a volunteer vest steps out in front of us, barring the way.

Not so fast, the old man croaks, shaky right hand raised, defiant.

Outta the way, pal, I say. The kids, they're huddled up behind me, looking over their shoulders and no doubt wondering what the heck this guy's up to. You seen what's going on in there? We gotta get outta here. You should too.

I've been watching you, buster, the old man says, fumbling for a walkie-talkie that's clipped to his vest. Buddy waves his free hand around in a big circle. This is all your fault. You won't get away with it. Not on my watch.

Listen, I tell this hundred-some-odd pounds of frail bone and withered flesh standing between me, the kids, and the parking lot. I dunno what you're talking about. But we're getting outta here. Pronto. So step aside, please.

No can do, the old man says, shaking his head like he's sad about it. Like he's sworn to a solemn oath that he must now uphold, instead of occasionally directing zoo patrons the way to the pissers. Old man pushes the walkie-talkie's talk button and gurgles, Dispatch, I've got a live one here.

Back in the zoo somewhere, that old tiger roars. The kids push in close behind me. There's a lady pushing a stroller barreling down the road over my shoulder, headed our way.

Dad, the boy goes, pulling at my shirt. What are we gonna do?

Don't worry, I mutter back. I take hold of both their hands, give each one a long squeeze. Just follow my lead.

The old man, he's still mumbling into the radio. I whisper to the kids, On three, OK? The kids nod their heads, eyes wide. In for a penny, in for a pound. For a moment, the past few years have been erased. It's like I've never failed them, ten feet high and golden this whole time.

OK, I say. One, two, three, GO!

The old man, he jumps, fumbling the radio as I make a break for it, kids following close behind. I drop my left shoulder, feint as though I'm gonna try to get past him on that side. He bites, shuffling off to his right. At the last second, I shift back the other way, hauling the kids through the gap the old timer's left wide open. We push through the gate, the parking lot spread wide open before us. We'd made it!

But then I feel my feet come out from under me. What the shit? I hit pavement, hard. I try to roll out of it, but no dice. I look down at my feet, figuring they're caught in the gate somehow. But it's the old man. He's tripped me up with his cane. He's fallen too. I worry for a second that he's maybe broken his hip, but the old bastard is pawing at my sneakers, trying to get a grip. I look back up at my kids, who have caught on to what's happening.

Run for it, I holler at them, tossing my car keys to my daughter.

She's almost twelve, and tall for her age. The Toyota's an automatic, and she's always been a quick study. If she don't know how to drive already, she'll figure it out quick I'm sure.

My daughter, she catches the keys, no sweat. But the kids, they hesitate. I can tell they want to come pull me loose from the old man's clutches. But that'll just slow us all down.

Get outta here, I yell, waving them off. I don't mind taking the heat for letting those animals loose, but I don't want my kids mixed up in it, too. Christ. I'd never hear the end of it. Besides, if the kids can get the car started, I figure maybe I can catch up to them near the exit, once I lose the geezer.

The kids, though, they're still lingering. They don't wanna leave me. It's Father's Day, after all.

I love you, I holler, waving 'em off again. But you gotta move it.

My daughter, she looks like she's about to cry. But she gets it. She's always been a smart cookie. Just like her mom.

I love you too, daddy, she calls, then turns and beelines it to the parking lot.

My son, he holds up a moment, like he can't decide what to do. Pushes the glasses back up his nose.

I'll catch up, buddy, I yell, trying to kick my feet out of the old man's death grip. Security's on the radio, hollering for backup. Promise!

Finally, my son starts moving his feet. But he's looking back at me with a crazy grin on his face.

See you soon, dad, he hollers, before turning to hoof it after his sister. Love you!

Makes a father proud, something like that.

Now, I know my goose is probably cooked here. This old guy just won't quit. I understand it could be a while before the kids and I have another chance to get together. If their mother ever lets me near 'em, I'll have to come up with somewhere else to take 'em, that's for sure. But what the hell? You gotta roll the dice once in a while if you wanna win big.

And that look on my kids' faces, running down the main drag at the zoo laughing and grinning just like the kids they are while all those animals are passing us every which way, the Bengal roaring off in the distance? That's joy, friend. Fleeting, sure. But pure. What father wouldn't want that for their kids?

THE COAT

"Hell yes," Dave answered when his cousin Lisa asked if he'd like to see something weird.

Dave followed Lisa off the deck and back to where the cars were parked as the sun was sinking in the west, cutting through the trees in brilliant bars of gold. Down by the lake, children shrieked and splashed in the late-afternoon heat. He was sick of answering his family's questions about his dumb job and why his girlfriend, Sandy, hadn't made the trip out because they'd "sure like to meet her." Something weird, whatever it was, would be a welcome change.

"Dave," Lisa's husband Rick said, glancing back as he rummaged through boxes of clothing in the back of their Golf with one hand. "Wait till you get a load of this . . ."

Rick and Lisa ran a vintage clothing store, and Rick had just finished a buying trip to the small-town thrift shops in the area. Dave kept up with their latest finds on Instagram. While he could appreciate their taste, he didn't quite understand how the market for such kitsch actually functioned profitably. But what did he know?

"Here we go." Rick put aside his beer and pulled out an old suitcase from beneath the mound of clothes. Carefully, he laid it down on the bed of dried pine needles that covered the rocky ground. Lisa and Dave leaned in to see as Rick popped open the brass clasps. A mosquito buzzed in Dave's ear.

Rick checked over his shoulder to see that nobody had drifted over from the deck. Out on the lake, a big engine whined. Then he opened the suitcase and delicately reached inside, pulling out a black fur coat.

"Feel it," Rick said in a hushed voice, holding the coat out before him as though it were an offering.

"What is it?" Dave asked, running the long, twisted strands of jet-black hair between his fingers. It was soft, almost delicate, yet also thick and grainy. The lining was torn, the pelt cracked at the left shoulder. The thing had to be a hundred years old. "Bear? Fuckin' otter or something?"

"No," Rick answered with a conspiratorial grin, brown eyes glinting. "Gorilla."

The hairs on the sleeves danced in rays of sinking sunshine. Repellant as he felt a coat made from the skin of man's closest evolutionary relation *should* have been, he was curiously, undeniably drawn to it. What would it be like, he wondered, to pull a gorilla's skin over his own?

"Can I try it on?"

***

Later that night, Dave slept fitfully while his younger cousin Frank snored like a log on the bunk beneath him. In the morning, he couldn't shake the feeling that he'd been dreaming, dreaming of gorillas in the damp city streets, their deep bellows and shrill cries echoing off the drab gray buildings. Dreaming he was one of them, proud, noble, and strong.

After returning home following the long weekend festivities, the dreams seemed to follow him. Dave also found himself thinking about the coat more and more as the days of summer flew by. Sitting in his car, in his office, chewing a sandwich at lunch, he thought of the weight of the coat on his shoulders, the way the hair glistened in the setting sunlight. How it felt between his fingers, so unexpectedly soft.

When he and Sandy first saw each other after the long weekend, they spent the night fucking with vigor that left the both of them breathless, sweating, exhausted.

"What's gotten into you?" Sandy asked, red-faced after their second round. Lately, if they did it at all they did it sporadically and in a desultory, mostly missionary manner. "You're like a goddamn animal!"

"Dunno," Dave panted, surprised with his own virility. "Must have just really missed you, I guess?"

Yet as he lay next to Sandy, raw, spent and slipping towards sleep after their third round, Dave suspected the uncharacteristic verve he displayed had something to do with the dreams he'd been having where he was a silverback gorilla roaring into the darkness.

That it had something to do with the coat.

***

"Yo, careful with those clasps there, Davey," Rick said.

Startled, Dave realized he had begun to finger the delicate, finely crafted clasps that ran down the front of the coat, from the neckline to the waist, slowly doing them up one by one. The coat fit surprisingly well, though a little tight across the shoulders, the arms perhaps an inch too short. Otherwise, it was perfect. Dave felt as though he could wear the coat forever, summer heat be damned.

"What's something like this set you back?" he asked Rick.

"Hard to say," Rick shrugged. "Got a super sweet deal. Estate sale outside of Detroit Lakes. Lady had no idea what it was. Goddamn, eh? Thing's, like, basically fuckin' priceless, right?"

Rick maintained that while it *technically* wasn't illegal to buy the pelt of an endangered animal, had the lady who'd sold it to him known what it really was, she could have found herself in some hot water.

"Don't ask, don't tell, man," he'd said. "Fucked eh?"

Dave just nodded, lost in a misty day dream.

***

At work, Dave became increasingly distracted. When he was in front of the computer, he found himself drifting into Google searches, keywords: "gorilla + coats." He'd wade through fashion op-eds decrying some celeb or another for sporting one to some event or other, animal rights sites calling for the heads of anyone who'd even think to buy or sell one, blogs extolling the virtues of faux fur over the real deal, whatever, so long as there were photos of the coats in question embedded in the post.

Hours disappeared. He shuffled between work and home in a haze, thinking, coveting the coat. Evenings in his empty apartment it was more of the same. Dave stared at the blue screen as light faded from the summer sky outside, imagining how it would be to live within the gorilla's skin, to live as a silverback among the misty mountains.

As August long weekend approached, Dave casually mentioned to Sandy that it might be fun to take a little day trip to the zoo.

"Why?" Sandy scoffed.

"Why not?" Dave suggested, feigning nonchalance. Of course, he hadn't told her about the coat. He couldn't exactly place or explain the fascination the coat held to himself, let alone to Sandy. Instead, he kept his budding obsession private. He wasn't sure she'd understand. Then again, she hadn't really seemed to notice, anyway. During the week, she was either working, at her parents' place, or out with her friends. The few hours they did spend together over the weekend mostly involved eating, sleeping, bickering, and the occasional fuck. "When's the last time you went to the zoo?"

Sandy had rolled her eyes, yet when Saturday morning came around they drove to the zoo. The day was a hot one, the air at the zoo humid and pungent. Dave and Sandy saw bears, wildcats, muskox, all manner of exotic rodents, and a tiger lolling in the shade. There were monkeys—zany macaques and bored chimps—but no gorillas.

On the way home, after a lunch of chip truck burgers and fries, Sandy coyly suggested they pull over into a nearby park so they could make it, hot and heavy, in the back seat.

"How about a bit of that jungle love?" she said.

But Dave just shook his head and kept driving.

"Not really in the mood," he sulked.

***

Later that night, as Sandy lay sleeping while the oscillating fan moved the muggy air in the apartment around, Dave lay wide awake. Sure, they'd gotten it on, but the spark that had been there that first night back from the lake and those first few nights that had followed had already faded away.

Hours later, when Dave finally fell into a fitful, sweaty sleep, he dreamed yet again of great apes and mountains shrouded in mist, of big guns blazing and the belching of a steam-engine chugging full throttle up a dark river.

When Sandy left the next morning, back to her parents' house, Dave shuffled into the shower, hoping a cool blast off would clear his muddy mind. Instead, he wondered if gorillas ever luxuriated in the midst of a tropical downpour. Did they enjoy the respite from the sweltering jungle heat? Or was it just another meaningless change in the weather they had no choice but to endure? Dave rubbed shampoo into his hair, thought about the soft, thick gorilla hair that had hung from his arms, the odd golden lock that caught the fading sunlight off the lake.

He wondered if Rick still had the coat.

Why, it occurred to Dave, don't I just ask him?

A moment later, he sprang from the shower, leaving the cold water running. He grabbed his phone, scrolled madly through his contacts until he found Rick's number. His wet thumb hovered over the screen.

What would Rick and Lisa think of him, Dave worried fleetingly, obsessing over some dusty old coat?

What did he care, though? Really. He only ever saw them once or twice a year, anyway.

If he had the coat, what did he care what Rick or Lisa, or Sandy or anybody, thought of him? At the end of the day, he would be the king of the jungle, or as close to it as you could expect to become in muggy old Ottawa after 5 p.m. What does the noblest of beasts care for the opinions of others?

Not a goddamn bit.

Fuck it. Dave pressed the green call button.

"Dave?" Rick's voice crackled after a couple rings. "What's up my man?"

"That coat," Dave said, stumbling over his words in haste. Shampoo ran down his face, burning his eyes. "The gorilla? I know you said you can't, like, sell it or whatever. But I was hoping, maybe, we could, like, come to an arrangement or something?"

"Oh man," Rick laughed. "That old thing? Sorry bud. No can do."

"Why not?" Dave stammered. "I got money. I'll pay whatever."

"No, no," Rick continued. "It's not that. I don't have it anymore."

"What?" Despite the swampy heat of his apartment, a chill ran up Dave's back. "But you said, you know, you couldn't sell it, or whatever. Right?"

"Didn't sell it. Made a trade with a buddy of mine out west. He collects weird shit. Freaky stuff. Had him in mind when I first picked it up. Sorry man."

Dave stood staring in his bathroom mirror. A pathetic, pale and mostly hairless monkey stared back at him. His bottom lip quivered.

"Dave?" Rick's tinny voice chimed from the forgotten phone in his hand. "You still there, buddy? Dave?"

Tears ran down Dave's cheeks, softly at first, then following fits of wracking sobs. The tear had nothing to do with the shampoo in his eyes. Nothing whatsoever.

OGOPOGO LIVES

It was Canada Day by the big lake and everyone was right fucked up.

After the fireworks show on the beach wrapped up, the crowd took to the streets. Things were getting messy. Drunk girls held on to each other, hiking mini-skirts up around hips to piss off the wharf into the black waters below, howling. One fell in, came up splashing, laughing. Muscle dummies squared off in the road, blocking traffic, letting the blood out of each other. Strip clubs up and down the lakeshore were packed, dancers raking in the money hand over fist. A police helicopter circled above, spotlight illuminating scenes of depravity that would make Bosch blush.

Kevin and his buddies were right in the middle of it. Floating on waves of psilocybin and pilsner, they drifted from a backyard barbecue and booze up just south of the highway over to the beach to take in the beautiful explosions, then aimlessly along among the throng as it poured back through downtown. One buddy disappeared into a dance club, one popped into the peelers, another just drifted off, mumbling at trees and trying to open locked cars he thought might be his, until Kevin was alone again, swaying slightly in front of a street punk busking for change.

"We're gonna be rich," the big boy in patched pants and sleeveless jacket sang, voice gravelly as the arid valley soil all around. The battered guitar he strummed upside down had the words "Mr Awesome" scrawled in sharpie along the body. "Because the Ogopogo lives."

"Fuckin rights," Kevin mumbled, tossing the dude a buck before shuffling off, away from the echoing horns and sirens and drunken hollering towards a park by the water. The song's expression of hope buoys him onward.

Love is in the air.

Kevin can smell it. Sees it everywhere his footsteps take him, though not for him. Squirrels chase each other up around and over the branches of an American elm. Crouched on a mattress in an alley, a man leans away from a dry handy to vomit on the hot concrete. Further up, among the aging bungalows, a couple are full on fucking on the hood of a beige Toyota Corolla.

The road crosses a stream dried up in the summer heat. Little more than a ditch, really, full of trash and brambly weed and emanating a foul stank. How many such streams, sometime and former means of shunting moisture down the valley towards the big sink, had been paved right over or rerouted beneath concrete? Fuck only knows. But Kevin follows the one he's stumbled across west until he hits beach access.

Blessedly, nobody's fucking here. Visibly, at least. Dogs barking, Kevin flips his rotting kicks off, letting the grimy sand squelch dryly between his toes. He sits down where the black water laps the shore, shoves his feet into the cool wet void with a deep sigh.

That's the ticket.

Sounds of the city drift up the lake. The chopper, sirens, the odd car alarm blaring, the drone of ceaseless traffic becomes background chatter, white noise.

"We're gonna be rich," Kevin hums, sipping warm soda and rum, wide eyes staring out at stars rippling off the water. "Because the Ogopogo lives."

The lake is deep.

The lake is long.

The lake is wide.

Must be plenty of places for a big bastard fish or whatever to frolic or layabout down there. How long he stares, sitting there, Kevin doesn't know nor care to find out. He's content, watching the interplay of light and dark, wondering if a prehistoric beast from the deep will emerge before his eyes or not. Isn't counting on it. Not disappointed when it fails to appear. Knows, if he were Ogopogo, he sure as shit wouldn't be showing his face on Canada Day. No way Jose. Save that for the solstice. Or the equinox. A full moon, or maybe the new? Some pagan holiday, anyway, as ordained by the stars or the moon or whatever calendar the pagans planned their parties by. The alignment of the planets, perhaps?

Kevin wonders if Ogie ever gets lonely, cruising the depths of this primeval waterway? Is there a mate it has longed for, over the ages, who was lost, cut off in some upper channel, when the glacial flood waters receded? Does it pine, lowing in an age-old subsonic language, beneath the waves, for its long-lost lover?

There's no way they'll ever be reunited, Kevin knows. But does Ogie? Has it accepted eternal solitude, or does it hold out, hopelessly, for a miracle? Ten thousand years is a long time to pine.

How does a monster as ancient as Ogie measure the passing of epochs?

Such solitude has Kevin feeling blue. Where has his love gone? Over the hills and far, far away. Of that he is sure. What drove that love from him? Something akin to a change in climate, personal if not meteorological. Way it goes, he knows. The way it goes.

Kevin takes a long pull off a warm drink, smacks his lips, and gets back up to his feet. The sounds of the city have diminished, but not disappeared. Hours remain before the sun pokes above the valley to the east, though the sky is beginning to lighten.

To the north, a small mountain looms. A provincial or regional park of some sort—he's never really been clear—with dusty trails snaking up to its peak. Kevin's climbed it before, sober as a judge and high as a kite and most everywhere in between. From the top, eyes can see far and wide before the lake swings out of sight behind the hills in either direction.

Whistling the beggar punk's tune, Kevin figures he may as well climb. See what he can see. Should Ogie or something of similar lost mythology pass by in the early light before dawn, would not a shadow conceivably be visible from such a vantage?

It's a holiday, after all. He is off. Up, up, whistling away.

A LAKE WEDDING

The mother of the groom got up and gave a speech as unhinged as any I'd ever heard. Then the father of the bride got up and topped her. They went on about kings and queens, elves and beggar thieves. Their children saints who deigned to walk among us. As though we didn't know them.

Dinner came and went. Further toasts and roasts delivered. My wife was pregnant, while I'd been drinking pretty heavily since the early afternoon. I'd also eaten a handful of mushrooms a buddy'd palmed me before dinner, and they were coming on strong. I rode them out as best I could, until I couldn't any longer.

When the dance floor opened up, we let loose; bodies moving, a seething mass of drunk aunts and uncles, lifelong friends and former lovers. There was a lot of history out there, popping and locking, years like bodies slipping and sliding loosey goosey all over the place.

Wine bottles were passed indiscriminately, hand to mouth and back again. The volume inside the big white tent—the laughter and catching up, the gossiping and well wishing and incoherent backbiting babble—just kept climbing. The world buzzed on a cellular level.

The dance floor cleared. Some kid cousin did the worm. Time writhed, stretching out beyond any fashion of fathoming as the God Emperor with an undercut bent the world to their senseless wiggly will.

Outside, the din echoed as though from a far-off cavern, some lost world. Marijuana made the rounds. The stars sparkled, bright pinpricks against the void, when you stepped far enough away from the lights of the tent to see them. A waxing moon, nigh on full, fired the sun's light back bright enough to shade the night as it climbed above the shimmering water.

Bodies I'd known over the years, intimately or otherwise, began streaming down the lawn towards the shore, shedding shoes, jackets, shirts, dresses, slips, and pants as they went. Not like it was the first time something like this had happened. It was a lake wedding, after all.

Though I was drawn by their atavistic howling, my own animal drive and the history that bound us, I ventured no further than the rocky beach. Instead I stood staring out towards the far shore, longing and revulsion rising and falling like a poorly mixed cocktail in my guts, as their tanned limbs and luminescent nethers, brown blonde red black gray hair soaked, splashing, thrashing among the waves, became a fleshy kraken, some lost beast of the deeps before my wide and bloodshot eyes.

"Peligro, amigo," I heard someone call from behind me. "Peligro."

I could have sworn, then, that I was in Mexico, eighteen again, a lifetime yet ahead. The water lapped the shore, pulling at me over the years. The heat of the southern sun shone on my face, the passion and fearlessness of youth coursed through my veins. The waves swelled, crashing about my knees.

But I wasn't in Mexico. I wasn't eighteen, living each day with abandon. Had I ever been?

Jolted half-sober, the unstoppable years rushed back upon me in an instant. I looked back over my shoulder, knee deep in the frigid water.

My wife stood, waving from the shore.

Dripping, I ambled unsteadily up the bank towards her as the "Boot Scootin' Boogie" warbled out from the tent. Laughter echoed over the water like the mad baying of loons while long-dead stars tumbled on, cold in the empty heavens.

GORD'S STILL RIGHT PISSED

MOTHERFUCKER TOSSED A TEN-PIN bowling ball through neighbour Gord's windshield by mistake there. August long weekend. I mean, motherfucker had every intention of tossing it through the windshield. Only Gord's Aerostar wasn't the intended target. Oh ya, motherfucker'd been drinking. Everybody was. Long weekend and all. No excuse. But what ya gonna do? Motherfucker figured buddy was stepping out with his ex. Probably was. But she's free to do what she wants, right? Live laugh love eh? So, buddy says something and motherfucker goes off. Fuckin *right* off, bud. Someone kept 'em from fighting there out front of the Inn. Sent motherfucker packing one way, buddy stumbling back into the bar—thank Christ—or who knows what woulda happened. Remember last time? Anyways, motherfucker fucks off. Only, he's back an hour later with the bowling ball. Dunno where he got it. No idea. Don't wanna know. Gord, he was sleeping, passed out hard, at the time. Shitty news to wake up to. No fuckin doubt. He's insured, though. Sure. But there's your deductible right fucked. Nevermind explaining to insurance why motherfucker put a ten-pin bowling ball through the windshield and all. Gord's still right pissed about it. Oh ya. Big time.

THE NIGHT THE FRIDGE FUCKED UP PETE'S CAR

LOOK, WE ONLY THREW THAT FRIDGE off the balcony because the landlord said it was cool.

When we called him up back in June we told him, Man, this fridge you set us up with conked out. All the food's fucked. We didn't tell him whoever got the last beer before passing out the night before had left it open. It was a matter of time, really. Thing was old as fuck to begin with. We asked him, What are you gonna do about it?

Don't worry about it, he said. I'll be by later this afternoon.

Next day, he rolls up to the parking lot out back in a rusted-ass GMC with a new-to-us fridge in the back. A couple of us climbed up and got it out. He left a dolly and a frayed bungee cord and wished us luck hauling it up the rickety wooden staircase to the two-bedroom apartment the four of us had rented off him for the summer.

What do we do with the old one? someone asked. We all looked up at the dead fridge standing sentinel up on the porch behind us.

Landlord, he just shrugged. The rent was like six hundred bucks a month, no goddamn AC, and the place stunk like Subway all day every day. What did he care?

Wait for a quiet night, he said, hopping back in behind the wheel. Nobody around, just toss 'er off the side. Lemme know, I'll come pick 'er up.

That old fridge, some shade of tan, sat out on that porch the rest of June, all of July, and into August before we finally got it together to get it gone. It was a Saturday night. Some shitty punk bands were playing in the bar across the street. They were bad, sure, but they were fast and loud and it got us fired up. Between sets, a half dozen of us stepped out to get high out back of the pizza place, and someone suggested we toss the fridge. Why not?

We finished off the bag of salvia, and when the singer counted off the start of the next set, we slipped across Manawaka Boulevard and climbed those rickety stairs to our place.

The parking lot below was empty, other than Pete's car, which was parked at the foot of the staircase. Otherwise there was nothing but gravel clear to the backroad and the marsh or swamp or whatever was in behind there.

Pete was inside the apartment, tripping on shrooms and watching surf videos. We told him he might wanna move his car. He didn't wanna.

Think you could just, like, clear it? he wondered, scratching his bare belly.

We all went back outside, except Pete. Pete stayed on the couch, pupils wide as saucers. He was fucked. The six of us picked up the fridge, easy peasy. Felt light as a feather. We set it back down. Someone hocked a loogie off the porch, sent it sailing into the night to land in dust somewhere way beyond Pete's car. Then we all went back inside and told Pete, We'll clear your Corolla, no sweat.

Shiiiiiiiit, Pete giggled, rolling himself off the couch onto the floor then somehow into an upright position. Guess I gotta see this.

Back out in the darkness, we picked up the fridge again with ease. Pete took up position by the rail.

Guys, he mumbled, as though trying to convince himself that he ought to be giving the situation at hand more careful deliberation while falling far short of the mark. You think there's any fuckin aliens up there watching right now?

Hope so, someone said. They're in for a treat. Count us down, Petey.

Pete obliged. When he hit that go mark, we all stepped forward and heaved our load into the void.

Man, that sucker flew. Like, right fuckin sailed through the warm August air, clearing the Corolla with an ease that seems hard to believe, looking back on it now. Hell, we coulda lined a couple low-list sedans up alongside it and that Frigidaire would have cleared them all. No problemo.

It was the landing that fucked it all up.

When those 400 pounds or whatever that old beast weighed came crashing down the doors blew off on impact. The freezer door spun through the air, slamming into Pete's passenger side door so hard it blew the window right out. The main fridge door nearly missed the car, but it managed to clip the back end, smashing the tailight to bits and ripping the back fender off. The fridge itself just crumpled, hissing freon into the night.

Oh shit, we cried, mumbled, or sighed. Except for Pete.

My car, Pete mumbled. I'd like to think he wasn't crying, but he probably was. Pete was an emotional guy at the best of times. You guys totally fucked up my car, man.

Don't worry, somebody said. We'll fix it, Petey. No sweat.

I'd like to think it was me, laying a reassuring hand on Pete's shoulder, letting him know we had his back. We'll figure this out, buddy. We'll tell insurance some kids fucked it up. Fuckin rights we will.

But I was probably just staring up into the stars, wondering if any aliens had actually been watching or not. Had we brought shame upon our world by our actions, or had we pro-vided a fleeting moment of joy to our intergalactic visitors?

I like to think they got a kick out of it, anyway, buzzing around up there just giggling. Pete would have wanted it that way, probably.

THE WIND? I SEEN IT ALRIGHT

THE WIND, THE WIND, THE GODDAMN WIND off the big lake has been roaring over us for days and nights on end; sending wave after countless wave crashing into the rocky shore; howling over the roof, slapping hard at the windows, and cutting in under the eaves and through the cracks in the walls and the gaps under the doors in this dusty old summer cottage we're bunked up in.

"It'll be fun," my wife and I told each other, leading up to our vacation. "Kids'll love it."

By and large, they have. What's not to love about the lake? They've even made some beach pals among the summer people. I'm the one who's struggling.

We'd rented the cottage—for a pretty penny, I might add, determined as we were to give the kids a real lake experience this summer—through an acquaintance, the brother-in-law of a lawyer I play squash with once a week. While he'd described the place as having a "rustic, old school vibe," I made the mistake in assuming he was being falsely modest.

Not so.

I'm sure it was nice enough, in its day, located as it is on a little northwesterly facing point with a great view of the big lake out the front. But the path leading down into the property from the gravel road above was nearly overgrown, bush and tall trees crowding up against the cottage, as though to reclaim it. Inside, there were spiderwebs in all the corners and daylight showing through the roof like so many stars on a moonless night.

"I'll get my guy to swing by and throw some tar up there," was what the lawyer's brother-in-law told me when I brought it to his attention. "Should do the trick."

We settled ourselves in that first afternoon without further trouble. The day was clear, the air hot and humid and full of the sounds of summer revelry all up and down the beaches. The sun shimmered off the lake like silver. Silver turned to gold as the afternoon waned into early evening. After we got the kids to bed, the wife and I sat out on the deck to watch the burning red sun set across the lake.

"Cheers, my dear," I said with a satisfied smirk. We tinkled our goblets of shiraz together, scattered clouds aflame in hues of purple, pink, and orange, toasting our good fortune and the ten vacation days that lay ahead. "To a wonderful couple weeks at the lake."

"Cheers, big ears," my wife replied with a half drunk chuckle. "We've earned it."

The next day, a sunbaked handyman in cut-off shorts and Birkenstocks showed up with a ladder and a bucket of tar to mend the roof.

"Should do," the beach bum said with a wink, shrugging the ladder up over his shoulder after he'd finished up on the roof. "Enjoy your stay now."

The wind picked up shortly after the man left. It hasn't let up since.

The strip of sandy beach in front of our cottage—which I should add had been a big selling point—was all but obliterated by the waves crashing up and over again and again and again and again. And again.

Undeterred, we packed up and hauled them across to the beach on the south side of town, which was protected from the waves by the town's new concrete pier. The place was packed, families everywhere. It was fine, as far as a day on a crowded beach goes. The kids loved it, I sunburned my shoulders and bald spot something fierce, and my wife kept chatting with people she knew, somehow or other, as they came and went. Those people, summer people up from the city, would inevitably ask us how long we were up for and where we were staying.

"There, eh?" they'd respond, or something similar, phony smile faltering just a little when we told them. "Well. So nice to see you, anyways."

Getting the kids all the way back to the cottage, cranky and covered in sand, in time for dinner was a chore in and of itself. Afterwards, dishes done and kids asleep in bed, the wife and I went out to view the sunset, but were quickly driven back in by the wind.

"Sun'll set again tomorrow," my wife shrugged, filling our wine glasses to the brim before we settled into the cottage's musty old couch.

But the wind was worse the next day, somehow worse still the next. It kept up steady, throwing waves up against the shore beneath the cabin and driving us across town each day if we wanted to hit the beach. Which, invariably, was where the kids wanted to be from the moment they woke up till we dragged them, suntanned and sandy, home for dinner.

Breezy as the days were, the wind seemed to really save itself for when the sun began to sink. Then it would howl all night. I couldn't seem to catch a wink, no matter how much I put back to drink between happy hour and hitting the sack each evening. No matter if the wife and I had a roll around or not. No matter. The wind kept blowing.

"I can't stand it," I complained to my wife one morning, as bacon splattered in the cast iron pan. "It's like it's trying to drive me bonkers."

"So it's a little breezy," my wife shrugged. "Put some earplugs in or something."

"Where does the wind come from anyway?" the oldest kid asked, scarfing down bacon.

"Nowhere," I answered shortly. "Everywhere. All over."

"You seen the wind, daddy?" the youngest inquired.

"Oh, I seen it alright," I boasted, chuckling foolishly to myself.

"Then what's it look like?" the oldest asked.

"Doesn't look like anything," I snapped. Kids can be such smartasses. "Just dumb air."

That night I couldn't sleep. Not a goddamn wink. Again.

The wind found ways to blow in through the cracks in the cottage walls, rustling newspaper, threadbare drapes, and dust. I thought I could hear our towels and swim trunks snapping off the line, pictured them tangled up in trees, high and out of reach.

While our items from the line were intact the next morning, we discovered a large birch branch had not been so lucky, having been flung from its former home across the path that led up from our cottage to the road.

I called up the lawyer's brother-in-law. He made his way down in short order from his newer, roomier cottage south of the pier on a shiny new Schwinn beach cruiser. But when he saw the branch, the lawyer's brother-in-law just laughed.

"Does seem a bit windier over this side," he shrugged. "Not so bad, over where we are. I'll have my guy come by and cut this up here for ya this afternoon."

The beach bum who'd fixed the leaky roof cycled into the yard after lunch on a rusty old Sekine, toting a banged up

Husqvarna in one hand. As we stood around the fallen birch limb, I asked him if he could score me some weed, by chance. He looked like the type. I hadn't thought to hit the dispensary before leaving town. Hadn't even considered it.

"No prob, Bob," the beach bum told me with a wink. He dug into his pocket, pulled out a pack of smokes. "Got just what you need right here."

Buddy took a joint out of the pack, handed it over. I thanked him profusely, enthusiastically even, though my name's not Bob. Overpaid him for it, too, no doubt. But it didn't matter. I was desperate. Buddy just winked my way again, and fired up the chainsaw.

After the kids were in bed, I lit up out back of the cottage— with some difficulty, as you might imagine, on account of the goddamn wind—for the first time in years, maybe. A long time, anyway. My wife politely declined to join me.

Pleasantly stoned, I spent the evening sipping wine, staring out over the waves as the sun sank in the west, wind whipping up and over me. Later, I did in fact fall fast asleep for what seemed like the first time in ages. I slept deeply, too, without dreaming. But in the middle of the night, in the darkest hours, I woke in a panic. I didn't know who or where I was. The gloomy cottage was an alien world until memory emerged from the fog of wine and weed. I lay back down, catching my breath. My throat was parched, my tongue felt like a mildewy old carpet. As I lay there, on the lumpy old bed next to my softly snoring wife, outside I could hear the wind whispering, snickering, occasionally howling in derision.

I spent the rest of the night tossing and turning. The wind was talking to me, whispering conspiratorially, but I couldn't make out the words. The wind, I knew, saw right through me. Who was I to think we could pass for summer people with this pricey, shabby two-week rental? The wind knew better.

That morning, after breakfast, the weather seemed to have improved. There was almost a sliver of beach out front of our place. I insisted we stick close to home that afternoon. The kids agreed without any fuss. I got down there with them wholeheartedly, tired as I was. We built castle after castle only to watch the waves claw them back into the water. No matter. We had the place to ourselves, and nobody wandered up to make idle chitchat. I burned a heretofore untouched part of my back, while my wife sat up on the deck and read a book. What more can you ask for?

By the time we climbed the sandy bank back up to the cottage, though, the wind had picked up again. By dinner, clouds began to roll in over the lake.

"Tut, tut," I tittered. "Looks like rain."

"Been awful dry lately," my wife shrugged, sounding uncannily like her mother. "Could probably use it."

But it didn't rain that night. Not until the next night; last night, as it was. The wind, of course, remained a constant, sky overcast from dawn till dusk, with rain and thunder forecast overnight. We stuck around the cabin, playing card games and working through a stack of musty old puzzles we found in a closet. After dinner, we cuddled up on the couch under a blanket and read *The Wizard of Oz*, though it felt almost macabre as the wind rattled the windows and howled under the eaves and through the branches of the massive trees surrounding the cottage.

"Could a twister really up and lift us away, daddy?" the youngest asked.

"No way, sweetheart," I bluffed, my voice lilting with false confidence. "Not much chance of a twister rolling over the water out there."

"Could the waves wash us away?" the eldest chimed in, having heard all about tsunamis and tidal waves in school or on TV or wherever kids hear things these days.

"No, no," I reassured, though honestly I had serious doubts. "It'd take more than a few big waves to wash this old cabin away."

It took the kids a little extra settling than usual. But once asleep, I poured myself a few fingers of Scotch and joined my wife in the front room. As she read her book, I stared out the dark windows as the rain began to fall. As the storm grew, so did my unease. My heart was pounding, my breath short. While the Scotch was nice—blended, but still—it did little to staunch the anxiety building up inside me.

Drink empty, I began walking the floor, peering out the windows, as though my bloodshot eyes could penetrate the wall of shadow smothering the cottage. Rather, the sounds of the storm only poured fuel on my wildest fears. The wind would rip the roof off the cottage, topple a centuries-old spruce over to crush the walls. Lightning would strike the old timber structure, burning us all alive. The waves would roll up over the banks, ripping into the sandy shore and pulling us all down into the lake, our drowned bodies pulverized among the rocky depths by the relentless churning of the water.

"Are you OK?" my wife asked, startling me so bad I let out a little squeak.

"Fine," I lied. "Just fine."

"You're not acting fine."

"It's just . . . windy out there." I shrugged, feigning calm. "Like, real windy."

My wife shrugged back, returned to her book. Maybe this was a bad idea, this brooding.

Maybe this whole vacation was a bad idea? But I couldn't help myself. Someplace with a hotel, a waterpark, everything easy and laid out, would have been nice, right? But here we are. Pacing, I circled the cottage, peering up into the dusty rafters for leaks that weren't there, for some sign that the weather was getting the best of the woodwork. My wife kept reading. I tried to settle in, to join her, again and again, but my eyes kept dragging themselves back up to the dark window-panes as they rattled away.

Hours later, now, my wife has gone to bed. But I'm still up, still staring out over the lake, watching the wind rip the clouds apart and smash them back together again. Rain pours down, waves splash back up again. Lightning forks ever closer, thunder booming so close the glass in the windows rattles. The cottage itself seems to shake under the onslaught, which has dragged on now well past midnight.

Of course, the wind blows on. And it will keep blowing long after this little vacation of ours that we scrimped and saved for so is over. Long after it is nothing but faint memories and a few photos in the cloud. Even those will blow away, one day, too. Like everything else.

The wind, the wind, the goddamn wind keeps roaring up over us, slapping hard at the windows, a pressure crushing in from everywhere at once. Resigned, I step out the front door, face the dark empty lake with arms open wide, rain lashing my face, soaking my t-shirt, my shorts. It's OK, I keep repeating as lightning flashes, thunder booms. It's OK.

SHOO FLIES

THE BOY WAKES ME UP in the middle of the night.

"Daddy," he'll whisper, crawling into bed next to me. "I'm scared."

"Come here," I'll say, wrapping the quilt around him. "Don't worry."

"Room's full of shoo flies," the boy mumbles, nearly asleep.

Any bug that flies is a "shoo fly" to the boy—he's only three—except maybe butterflies and bumblebees. For his own reasons, he's taken a dislike to the things. No small wonder. Can't stand them, myself.

"It's OK," I'll shush, as much for his benefit as my own, wide awake as I am and staring up at the ceiling. "Just a dream."

In the light of the day, we'll sit at the kitchen table, eating.

"Ugh," the boy says, waving his milky spoon through the air in front of him. "Get outta here, shoo fly."

Sure enough, a little something bobs around above the bowl of bananas. I'll reach out over the table, slowly, then smack my palms together. When I open my hands, I'll show the boy.

"Yuck," he'll say, making a face if I got 'em.

"Rats," if I missed.

When the boy's mother and I first started seeing each other, she was staying in a studio apartment above a bakery. Once I started spending the night, I'd wake to a big fat fly buzzing around my head, alighting on my face as the early-morning sun broke through the blinds. It disgusted me, but I was head over heels with her. Instead of suggesting she spend more time at my place—a rented room in the basement of an old boarding house on the other side of town—I doubled down.

"We should move in together," I blurted one morning, figuring she'd call my bluff.

"For real?" she said instead, grinning big in that way that showed her chipped eye tooth, brown eyes sparkling mischievously. "That'd be fun!"

Fun it was, for a while. We got ourselves a one-bedroom apartment in a decent little neighbourhood not far from the university, filled it with furniture from the Goodwill, got back into studying once the fall rolled around. Then she got pregnant. After the boy was born, neither of us went back, though we both planned to pick up our studies when time allowed.

Now she's gone. Gone, gone, gone. It's just me and the boy, now. And the shoo flies.

When we're sitting around, the boy and me, the sight of a fat housefly buzzing idiotically against a window sends my skin crawling. I've sent my morning cup of coffee or my evening beverage crashing against the linoleum when startled by the creepy touch of their legs on my skin.

"What's wrong?" the boy will ask, eyes wide with worry.

"Nothing," I'll mutter, stooping to clean up the mess. "Shoo flies."

When I was a boy myself, of about eight or nine, I had a little rabbit for a pet. Soft white fur, cornflower blue eyes. She'd put up with just enough cuddling so as to endear herself as a pet, hijinks and all, and not a moment more.

She could get nippy, though, if she set her mind to it. And that's just what she did one early autumn afternoon when I went to bring her inside and out of the Indian summer heat.

So I left her to sweat it out there for another hour or two before I brought her in just after dinner. Next morning, I went in to give her a squeeze before heading off to school, but when I picked her up she wheezed in pain and nipped at me again.

"What's up girl?" I started asking, but then I seen just what was up. I dropped her back in her cage with a moan of my own and turned, hollering for my mother.

Bugs were crawling all up the back of the bunny, munching the poor thing up alive. My mother took the rabbit to the vet, who put it down, while I stayed home crying, horrified and disgusted.

Later, in the darkness, the boy will be waking me up again with his soft shuffle step and a whimper as he climbs into the big bed.

"There are no shoo flies here," I'll lie with a whisper.

"There," he'll insist, pointing up into the shadows. "The black buzzing things. Shoo flies."

I'll stare up into the far black corners of the room, which does indeed seem to buzz around, like a negative of static on a TV screen. I know it's nothing, the absence of light or something in the shadows, but I don't know how to explain it.

"It's nothing," I'll insist as soothingly as I can manage, while I lay there thinking.

I wish I'd held that rabbit close, that I'd soothed her, at least a little, in that final hour. But I never.

I wish I could have done something, anything, to keep the boy's mother here with us. But I couldn't.

I wish I could keep the shoo flies out of our goddamn apartment, but I can't even do that.

Of course I don't tell my three-year-old son any of this. What use would it be? Where would I even start?

"It's nothing," I'll lie, more for myself than the boy. "Shoo flies."

ROCK BOTTOM FEEDERS

FRANK WOKE SLOWLY, his head pounding along to the sound of water lapping against the rocky shore. Thousands of stars and a bright full moon shone through the darkness above, reflecting in twinkling waves across the water.

Moaning, dizzy, and nauseous, Frank blinked. He wasn't sure just where he was or what he was doing there, but his feet were wet and he felt a strange tingling sensation all over his body. Behind him somewhere, a babbling creek dumped water into the bay.

It all came back to him slowly through a haze of pain. He was forty-three years old and on the bender to end all benders, devastatingly hungover if not still wasted from the previous day's boozing.

Something, at some point, had gone wrong. Real wrong.

The last thing he could recall clearly, he'd been drinking in a bar not far from the ferry terminal. How much time had passed since then? Hours? Days? Frank did not know. He'd been drinking hard for weeks, since before he'd hopped on the Greyhound back on the prairies and headed west, redoubling his efforts to reach oblivion once he'd hit the coast. Time had begun to lose meaning.

When the web of deceit he'd been spinning for years came unwound and he'd finally and irrevocably fucked up everything in his life, he'd fled. Why stick around while the lake froze over and the walls and the bank and the long list of varied creditors he'd accrued over the past few years, who had yet to clue into the fact he was beyond broke, closed in? He'd always wanted to live between the mountains and the sea. If not now, then when? There would be no happy retirement in Frank's future, unless he won the lottery, and maybe not even then, if his soon-to-be-ex-wife had anything to say about it.

Diane had left him. Of that he was sure. However, he had trouble identifying just why, at the moment. The drinking, maybe. But who didn't like a cocktail now and then? Diane certainly did. And how. Most likely it had been the gambling, and no doubt the subsequent loss of their home and business. Yes, that was it. All the money they'd had was gone, along with the house, the restaurant, the truck, the boat, and the fifth wheel. The run of bad luck had started as a trickle before escalating into a full on fucking tsunami and then, bingo bango bongo, Frank and Diane were way beyond broke and wasn't that a surprise to Diane.

"I never want to see you again," she'd screamed from the porch of her mother's house when he'd stopped by earlier that fall, for one last-ditch effort to patch things up before adding, "You're a fucking disgrace, Frank!"

Then, she'd turned and slammed the door in his face, leaving him standing on the front step in the cold wind, alone.

They'd spent ten decent years together. The restaurant they'd run for the last seven, The Dock, had been a success. The dining room had commanded a beautiful view of the lake, with a menu that leant heavy on the seafood and nautical decor that catered heavily to the tourist crowd. Tourists who were happy to scarf down flash-frozen fish dishes while they dined out, a chance to forget their worries for the weekend and soak up the brilliant prairie palette on display (most evenings) between eight and ten. The locals were just happy to have a different place to wet their whistles for six months of the year that The Dock was open for business.

Neither Frank nor Diane had particularly liked seafood. That was just what The Dock had always served, and what the tourists who came back every year expected. Sure, Frank would admit he'd come to develop an unhealthy penchant for deep fried crab cakes, but that was incidental. The fact that The Dock was a surefire moneymaker which also featured a prominent lakeside lounge had been the prime selling features for both Frank and Diane.

"If we're going to be drinking on a patio all summer," Diane had said over innumerable drinks on countless occasions over the past seven summers, "we might as well be making money doing it."

When they'd first bought the place it had been a rundown fixture of the lakeside cottage community for decades. They'd got it for a bargain, thanks to small-town family connections and the previous owner's mounting and costly health problems. All they'd really done to the place was slap a few coats of paint on the walls and replace the cigarette-and-fried-fish-reeking carpet with industrial laminate. Over the years, they'd replaced pieces of the kitchen, but even then, they'd bought used equipment. As a secondary source of income for the couple, The Dock had been easy money six months of the year.

Now, though, the good times and the easy money were gone. Long gone. Their marriage was over and The Dock had new owners. Maybe the new couple would replace the basa burger with bison, but it didn't matter at all to Frank. They could turn the menu upside down or burn the place to the goddamn ground for the insurance money for all Frank cared. At least, he thought bitterly, he and Diane had never had kids.

Painful as it was to admit, Frank had gambled and lost every last cent and then plenty more on credit and he didn't have a goddamn thing to show for it. He'd always enjoyed putting a bet down on a football game, had bet the ponies when he'd had an opportunity. The slappers were bad enough, but he'd learned the hard way years ago to stay away from them, especially when he'd had a few to drink and felt like getting lucky.

In the end, online poker was his downfall. It was a slippery slope, and so easy to sluff off the losses when they only appeared on an electronic credit card statement for a card he'd taken out in their joint names for the express purpose of gambling online. A card that Diane had never known about, until its balance in full came due and Frank was forced to admit he had no way to pay for, as he'd already extended credit on every conceivable asset they owned.

Now, not two years after first logging on as DockDude69, Frank's divorce was proceeding through the lawyers, and he had no way to pay for his half of it. Instead, he'd hopped a Greyhound westward, disembarking at the end of the line before stumbling on to a ferry a few days later on the fumes of his rapidly diminishing MasterCard balance.

He'd crashed with his older brother Bob those first few days on the coast, in the nice old West End home he shared with his wife Sharon, who still looked as good to Frank at fifty as she did when he'd made a drunken pass at her a couple weeks before she and Bob were married twenty years earlier.

"Happy to have you," Bob had said, and he'd meant it, Sharon smiling patiently at his side. "Stay as long as you want to, bro. We'll have some fun."

But brother Bob had three kids who didn't need to find their sad old Uncle Frank snoring through a hangover on the couch every morning when they woke up to get ready for school. Bob hadn't said as much. No, Bob would never, but he didn't have to. Bob knew it. Frank knew it. And while Sharon, bless her, had never once mentioned the fumbling drunken fool he'd made of himself those twenty years earlier, Frank knew she hadn't forgotten, either.

After a few days on the couch, Frank had left a *Thank You* note on the breakfast nook table, helped himself to a fresh bottle of Bobby's finest single malt, and hit the road.

Now, here he was, lying on some miserably rocky beach in the dark. With some trouble, Frank rubbed his face with his gritty left hand, shooting pain down the arm well past the elbow. The smell of brine, rotting vegetation, and blood cut through the clouds of boozy stink he exhaled with every breath. A wave of nausea washed over him, like the waves lapping at his feet which, Frank realized through the haze, were bare. Where had his boots gone and why did it feel like his toes were being slowly flayed, cold little wet piggie by cold little wet piggie?

He'd met a woman that first day off the ferry, he remembered. Half cut, he'd waltzed into a restaurant by the harbour, sat down at a booth overlooking the sea, and ordered the oysters.

"Fresh?" he'd asked the waitress.

"You betcha," replied the robust redhead who didn't look a day over forty, though she may well have had a couple years on Frank.

"I'm in," Frank had said with a wink. "Let's do it."

The two had continued to flirt as Frank racked up his bill. He'd managed to get her phone number from her, which he dutifully called from the payphone at a pub she'd told him she might enjoy meeting him at for a drink after her shift was over. While he waited, he kept on drinking, ordering a lavish dinner of crab legs and a sirloin steak, rare, that he had to admit was above and beyond anything The Dock had ever served during his tenure as owner/general manager.

Carla, the waitress, met him an hour later. They'd spent the rest of the evening boozing at a pub up the road from the ferry terminal. He'd then spent the night naked and drunk, rolling and groping, fucking and sucking across the floor and futon in her one-bedroom apartment. When he'd awoken in the morning, she was off to work an early shift.

"Call me later, big boy," Carla'd said with a lascivious wink as she headed out the door. Frank had a shower, got dressed, and finished off the heel of whisky they'd left on the coffee table before heading back out to hit the nearest bar.

It had been Frank's first night with a woman who wasn't Diane in over a decade. Never once during their marriage had he strayed, sexually. Rather, when the two began to drift apart, Frank had found solace in gambling and online pornography, while Diane had taken to drinking ever more wine in the evenings. Occasionally, they'd come together in the bed they shared, and they almost always enjoyed those times together. But all the good loving in the world wouldn't bring back the money Frank had secretly blown chasing a run of good luck that never arrived.

The night with Carla had been fun, sure. But it had also been sloppy. Lying on the beach, every part of him awash with pain, Frank could not remember if he'd seen Carla again or not, because from the previous afternoon on, Frank's memories were blotto. If he had, he'd certainly said or done something to lose favor with the busty, red-haired waitress. Why else would he have stumbled down to the beach to pass out? Clearly, he had a long way to go if he were ever to get back into her, or any other lady's, good books again.

Shutting his eyes against the night, Frank groaned. His head pounded. Even the ground beneath him seemed to crawl. Good Lord. What a mess.

Could this be rock bottom? Had he finally hit it?

Frank opened his eyes again. Across the water, a red light blinked on and off, on and off in the darkness. Was it a buoy bobbing on the waves, or a signal light on a lonely island of rock? It didn't matter. What mattered was figuring out where he was and how he got there and what in the Christ was that nipping and gnawing he felt in his legs and arms and back?

Pushing himself up off his back, Frank felt a sharp crunching under his elbows and his palms, which preceded a flurry of sharp pains rippling up his arms.

"Oh my god," Frank croaked, eyes watering as he shuffled frantically upright.

The ground crunched beneath him while something needled him at every pressure point. He raised his hands up before his eyes and stared at them in the gloom for what seemed like a long time, but couldn't have been more than a couple seconds. Then he blinked his blurry eyes, and looked again to confirm that what he thought he'd seen was, in fact, what he had seen.

It was. There was no mistaking it, horrifying as it was.

Dozens of tiny crabs clung to the flesh from his shredded palms, their little legs moving helplessly in the moonlight, searching desperately for purchase.

Frank screamed.

Flailing, swatting, pin-wheeling his arms madly, Frank scrambled up off the rocky beach, which was crawling with shadowy crustaceans. The pain in his feet as they slapped against the rocky sea bottom obliterated any discomfort he'd experienced upon waking, hungover, on the beach only moments earlier.

Scrambling backward, Frank screamed again when he caught sight of his feet out of water, covered in a seething mass of miniature creatures. Though his feet were still submerged in the cold water, he could feel them biting, pinching, clawing their way up the flesh of his legs beneath his loose fitting cargo pants.

Frank fell back on his ass with a sickening crunch. He tried to brush the crabs off his arms and hands, but their claws and their tiny pincher-mouths, mandibles and maxillae, held tight. Worse, for every successful brush, the crabs that were knocked loose tore off strips of flesh as they fell to the rocky shore below, where they were joined by dozens, hundreds, thousands of their kind, all seething up from the sea.

"What the shit?" Frank babbled, his mouth tasting as foul as the bilge water of a frigate long left adrift to the currents.

For all the thousands of pounds of crab The Dock had sold over the seven years he and Diane had been at its helm, not one had ever come through the back doors off the supply truck live. They hadn't even come in their shell, but long processed into deep-fryer-ready cakes far removed from their wild, bottom-dwelling lives.

The only live crabs he'd ever seen were in the tank at the Superstore, or the one time he and Diane had gone to the aquarium, when they'd visited brother Bob and Sharon shortly after they'd first been married. He'd never even thought about them, outside of doing inventory or as a tasty treat, not once.

"Why?" Frank howled as he pushed himself upright once again, turning to run up the beach.

Why indeed, he wondered fleetingly, had something so terrible come upon him all at once? What drunken, woebegone romantic impulse had compelled him to stumble down to this beach to rest his booze-besotted head and not some crab-free back alley or park bench instead?

The night provided no reply to Frank's desperate query. Instead, his feet, bare, lacerated, and throbbing with pain, slipped on a large, slimy piece of cast-off kelp. He fell back down to the beach, cracking the side of his head against a barnacle-encrusted rock.

His vision blurred, eyelids unfathomably heavy, Frank made one last bid to get up and run. But his limbs seemed a million miles away, attached to some other body. A body, perhaps, that had never known the thrills and spills, the lofty peaks nor the festering lagoon-like depths of the problem gambler; a body that had never left the placid, uneventful shores of Lake Manawaka; one that had never fucked up a fine and good thing so utterly, so completely; one that hadn't hit rock bloody bottom, running in vain from facing up to the consequences of his actions; a body that wasn't, at that very moment, being made a feast for crabs.

And still they poured from the sea, swarming up ahead of the creeping tide, water glistening off their shells in the gloom like a million drops of rain on a flat, clear lake as their tiny legs skittered sideways over the rocky beach. Among their countless dime- and dollar-sized brothers and sisters emerged crabs the size of fists and rocks and small dogs and larger still from the waters, dripping and sparkling in the moonlight, headed ashore; claws clicking open and shut, open and shut, open and shut with mindless, mechanical certainty. Headed for Frank.

BAUER SELECTS

THERE WERE ONLY A FEW OF US left hanging around when the rink rat that cleaned the dressing rooms poked his bald head in and gave us the ten-minute warning. A lull fell over the damp, sweaty room as a final round of cold ones were cracked.

"Hey Del," Barry belched, breaking the silence. "You ever tell the boys here about ol' Eddie?"

"Nah," I grumbled, waving his suggestion away half-heartedly. "These guys don't wanna hear nothing like that."

"What's this?" Johnsy asked, as he pulled on his drawers and plopped back down onto the bench to sip his fresh brew. "You holdin out on us Del?"

"Come on," Barry needled with a wink and a grin. "Let's hear it. Gotta finish up these pops, anyhow."

Now, I've told the story plenty over the years, late nights in the dressing room or early mornings sitting in a boat waiting on the fish to bite. It ain't a happy story, though.

"You boys sure? This ain't no heartwarmer."

The boys all egged me on.

I stole a glance into the case of Busch Lights left standing by the garbage can in the middle of the room. There were a couple more holding it down. If we ran late, we could always leave the rink rat a pop or two for keeping him there so late on a weeknight. He might cuss us out, but he'd forgive us. I took a long sip off my beer and sat back.

"Alrighty then."

***

Years ago, I used to skate with a group of guys out of the old Manawaka Memorial Arena, a few years before the roof caved in on her back in '97. Good group of guys, lots of laughs, and even a couple decent hockey players in the mix, too. Not unlike you lot.

Back then, there was a guy by the name of Eddie Franklin who'd lace up with us every Thursday night. Eddie was a nice enough guy, sure. He wasn't great shakes or nothing, but he was another body you could depend on, and he almost always brought beer. He was built like a brick shit house, too; you couldn't get him off the puck without a bit of muscle. But he didn't move too fast out there. Not until that final season he played with us, when he got them new-to-him skates, that is.

They were pretty banged up, heavier by far than anything you'd find new on the market these days, and they was held together by mismatched rivets, shoe goo, and a pair of frayed red and black laces that he never did get around to swapping out. Sure, they didn't smell so great, but them Bauer Selects fit Eddie just right and his old pair of CCMs were in even worse condition. So Eddie figures, what the hell.

"Blades were rusted somethin fierce," I recalled him saying, as he showed them off for the first time. "Nothin a good sharpen couldn't cure, though."

Course, Eddie never knew them skates was haunted, cursed, or worse when he bought 'em, else he never would've paid the forty bucks for 'em in the first place.

144

First skate of the year, you could tell something was different with Eddie. He was just zipping around out there like a bat outta hell, even in warm-up. Come game time, Eddie's hungry for that puck. Starving, even. Usually, he'd follow the play—try to make the safe move. But now, boy, he's after that puck like it owes him money. A nice change, sure, if somewhat outta character. Little urgency ain't a bad thing, right?

But then, all of a sudden you can't get Ed off the ice, neither. And that wasn't never the case before. Sure, he'd get caught out on a bad change now and then. We all do. Some—lookin at you Barry—more than others eh? But it wasn't never a problem before, neither. Now, though, Eddie don't never want to get off the ice. We'd have to holler at him and rattle that gate like hell each time he come zipping by and hope to Christ his ears was open.

"Sorry boys," Eddie'd say, dropping to the bench all red-faced and outta breath, panting like a lumber cat in heat. "Feet've got a dang mind of their own over here."

Eddie kept up that way, too, as the season went on. We'd rib him hard, and he'd apologize up and down, but nothing'd change. He was even playing different out there. Eddie'd always been active on the rush and quick to back check, but like most of us, it wouldn't be wrong to say he could lack any real sense of urgency before then, particularly during those late-night ice times.

But now Eddie's charging after the puck, flying into the corners, Lord help anyone in his way. It was like something had got into him. The refs took notice, too. Big time. There's Eddie, who'd never logged more than the odd accidental tripping minor, sitting in the sin bin every game, knees bouncing in the box the whole while, anxious to get out and get moving again.

"Here he is," the boys'd chide when he set himself down in the dressing room after each game. "Lookin a lot like Tiger Williams out there, Eddie!"

"Sorry boys," he'd say with a shake of his head. "Can't seem to catch a break with the stripes these days."

Then he'd pull his sweater over his head, crack a beer, and sit there, belly hanging out with his skates laced up. Matter of fact, Eddie'd gone from being one of the first guys up and outta the room to dang near the last each night. And it wasn't like he was showering up and lingering till the beer ran out. No, he'd just sit there, skates on, just kicking it till the next team came by to use the room or the rink rat gave us the boot, then pull his gear off lickety-split and head home, sweaty as could be. He'd leave them Selects on long as he could, too.

It was around that time, must have been mid-October, before the weather really turned cold, that I got my first indication that something was up with Ed. I'd got out of the shower, was lounging in my towel while he was still fully dressed, he hadn't even bent down to unlace those Selects yet. He said he'd got himself into a regular Wednesday evening pickup game over Minnedosa way.

"Right on," I tells him. "Really getting your money's worth for them new skates, eh?"

"Sure, sure," was all he says. "Can't get enough, these days."

I didn't think much of it, until I was chatting with him a few weeks later—coulda been a month maybe, I don't recall, exactly. When I asked him how it was going with them pickup games, his eyes bugged out again.

"Good," he says. "Found myself a regular Monday evening game up in Dauphin, too."

"Christ," I says, figuring between the 'Dosa and Dauphin games, old Eddie's really putting the miles on his old F-150. I says as much to him, but he just shrugged.

"Yeah," Eddie says. "But what the hell. Gotta scratch the itch, right?"

Heck, there's nothing wrong with driving all over the Parkland to play pickup hockey. But the look in Eddie's eyes and the way he'd been acting on the ice made me feel like something was going on with ol' Ed. Something strange.

See, Eddie's antics on the ice had only increased, too. He wasn't just running after the puck, but running guys into the boards and generally making a menace of himself. One night, right around that time, he even got himself thrown out of a game. He'd never done nothing like that before. No way, no how.

"Jeez, Ed," I says after we all get off the ice twenty minutes later. "What the hell's gotten into ya?"

Eddie, he's sitting there with his sweater and shoulder pads off, but he hasn't touched his skates.

"Sorry, boys," he says, sounding like a broken record. "I dunno what happened. Kinda lost it out there, I guess."

"No shit, Sherlock," some joker says. "Tell us somethin we don't know."

But Eddie just shakes his head. I noticed then that he'd lost weight. Used to be Eddie's gut would hang out over his Coopers, but no more. Wasn't surprising, considering all the skating he was doing. But Eddie still had that crazy look in his eye, too. Sunk back into his head as they was like he was some sorta Halloween goblin. When most of the guys had showered and headed home, Eddie was still sitting there, half-undressed and looking regretful. After I towelled off, I grabbed a couple cold ones from the open cases in the middle of the room and sat myself down next to Ed.

"You alright, bud?" I asks him. "Something eatin' ya?"

He took the Coors I handed him without a word and cracked it.

"Shit, buddy," Ed says after taking a long pull off his Colorado Kool-Aid. "Guess I ain't been sleeping much."

"Work?" I asks. "How's things at home?"

"Nah," he shrugs. "Work's work. Same shit as always. Home's the same. Only . . . It's like, when I try to sleep each night, it's like I can't stop thinking about the last game. Or the next one. And when I do sleep, I'm dreaming I'm chasing the goddamn puck down the ice and the rink is like a dark tunnel that goes on and on and on forever. It's fucked, I know, but—"

Eddie trailed off, then, and took a long pull off his pop. I did the same. What else could I do? I figured there must have been more going on with Eddie, behind the scenes, but I've never been one to pry. Especially not in the dressing room after a tough loss. So I let it slide.

I missed the next couple ice times—out of town for work for one, sick for the second—but when I returned to the rink in early December, Eddie looked even worse, run ragged and then some. He took a couple penalties that evening, but managed to keep his cool, more or less, if I recall correctly. When we got to talking, after the game, I asks him how things was going out in 'Dosa and up in Dauphin.

"Stopped going," he says, dropping his eyes. "Too much driving. Been hitting up the ODR two, three nights a week, though. Ain't the same, but she's worth it just to get out for a skate."

"Sure," I says, not thinking nothing of it.

Found out later that Eddie'd been asked not to come back out to either the 'Dosa or the Dauphin games. Seems his new-found attitude on the ice was rubbing the regulars the wrong way. Truth be told I wasn't terribly surprised. But never having known Eddie to lie, it seemed kinda weird that he didn't just tell me the truth. Guess he was embarrassed, and rightly so. Again, I never asked Eddie about it, though I've often wished I had.

Talk about missing one hundred per cent of the shots you don't take, eh?

***

"Did Gretzky really say that?" Johnsy asks. "Or is that, like, an urban myth or whatever?"

The boys all groan. Barry tosses a tape ball across the room, which bounces off his shoulder. These young guys, sometimes they ain't so sharp upstairs.

"Jeez, just asking boys," Johnsy says. "Sorry Del."

I wave off the boy's apology, take the opportunity to wet my whistle, gather my thoughts. It's been a while since I talked about ol' Ed, though I don't reckon there's an ice-time that goes by that I don't think of the poor guy.

"Now," I says, making a show of setting my beer down. "Where was I?

***

Over the holidays, the lake froze over. Not that it didn't every winter, but this year, considering we didn't have much of nothing by way of snowfall, the entire lake froze clear and solid and smooth as a skating rink.

It was incredible, one of them once or twice in a lifetime sorta things. Games of shinny were going round the clock it seemed, down by the main beach, while people passed the puck and played games of keep-away that stretched out the length of football fields across that crisp, clear ice. You could skate from shore to shore, unfettered by boards or snowdrifts or anything but the odd crack to hop over here and there.

I was out there the afternoon of New Year's Eve with the wife and the kids all bundled up, just puttering about and having some fun. Christ, it was cold as cold could be, but there was dozens of folks out there, too, bundled up as we was and making the most out of it.

Eddie was one of them.

We was catching a quick breather, about a half a mile out from shore, about to make our way back in to call it a day and grab a hot chocolate, when he skated up out of the bright reflection of the low winter sun. I raised a gloved hand and hollered, "Hey Ed!"

"Del," Eddie wheezes, out of breath and then some as he hit the brakes, cutting a wide swoop in to stop up next to us. "Didn't see ya there in the glare!"

I got a good look at him, then, as he stood there sucking wind. He was sweating, despite the cold. And while his face was red raw from the wind and the exertion, the tips of his ears and the bridge of his nose was frozen white.

"Ya got yourself a touch a frostbite there, Ed," I says.

"Really?" Eddie says, wiping his forehead. "Jeez, I'm just sweating buckets. You can really pick up some steam out there in the open."

"No kidding," I says. "But you're gonna lose an inch of ear if you keep it up, bud."

Eddie shook his head, blinked a few times, as though in a daze. Then his eyes seemed to focus on something off in the distance, out in the middle of the frozen lake.

"Sure, Del," he says, before taking a couple strides towards shore. "Nice running into ya."

We headed on in ourselves after that. I didn't think of Eddie again until I seen him at the rink a few days later. By then, he's got the look of a red raccoon, face wind-burned and frostbit around the eyes, and his ears was bright as Christmas ornaments.

"Cripes, Ed," I says with a whistle. "Wind done bitcha something fierce, eh?"

"Yeah," Ed says, all sheepish, sitting there in his skates a half hour before icetime. "Didn't feel like nothing when I was out there. But I guess I got 'er pretty good."

"Darn tootin' ya did, dummy," some joker chimed in. The boys all laughed, of course. Looking back now, though, I can tell ya that shoulda been a big red goal buzzer flashing to let us know that things wasn't right with ol' Eddie, not one bit. Instead, we just got dressed and hit the ice like every other night.

It wasn't long after that we all learned that Eddie and his gal, Laurenna, had split. Word on the street was that things hadn't been going well for a while, and it all kind of fell apart over the holidays. I never got a chance to ask her about it, so I can't rightly say what happened between them. All's I know is it was a sad mess, the whole damn thing.

Course, that is neither here nor there. Fact remains that by the time February rolled around, Laurenna had her own place across town, while Eddie kept living in the house they'd once shared. He kept looking worse, too—thinner—his beer belly shrinking until it didn't even hang over his pants anymore. At the time we put it all down to a case of the blues. A few of the boys had been in similar situations, so they took to him in the dressing room, going out for beers after the game or tagging along with him for a little skate or shinny session.

Eddie took to spending more and more time out on the ice, and not just down at the community centre ODR, but hitting up the big empty lake on the daily, too, skating away the empty hours. Wasn't much snow that year, and when it did fall, there wasn't much of it. The municipality'd cleared off a big old patch along the lakefront for folks to keep skating on. Others, and I reckon Eddie was one of them, even cleared paths and little shinny sheets further out onto the lake.

Who could blame the guy?

Problem was, Ed was out on the ice when he had no business being there.

One night, during a bitter cold front at the end of February, the kind of cold where trees pop and the ice screeches beneath your blades, Eddie went out and frostbit his ears so bad he lost parts of both of 'em.

Now, I only seen Eddie alive again one more time after that, and he wasn't looking too good, let me tell ya. Fact, he looked downright haggard. Both ears—what was left of 'em, anyways—was all swole up something fierce. His face was gaunt from the weight he'd lost, bags dark as pucks under his ghostly blue eyes.

"Tough luck, Ed," I tells him, when I stopped by his place to see him. "Doing OK?"

"Sure, sure," Ed says. "Tough luck for the boys last week, too, I heard."

Our season had just ended, with a loss in the first game of our winner-takes-all-playoff, while Ed had been shut up in hospital, and we wouldn't be back on the ice until late September.

"We'll get 'em next year," I says, before cutting to the quick of things. "What the heck were ya doing out there, bud?"

Ed shrugged and took a moment to answer, staring at the table while he put his thoughts together.

"It was like I was dreaming," he says finally, looking me in the eyes. "It felt good to skate. But it was also like I just . . . had to. Like I had no choice. The more I'd push, the harder I'd go. Harder I'd go, the lighter I felt. I'd be charging up the ice, just skating, not even chasing the puck or nothin, I just kept skating and skating and skating and that felt like it was enough."

I didn't say nothin. What was there to say?

"That might not make sense," Ed says with a sad, empty chuckle. "But that's how it is. Or was, I guess. You follow me, Del?"

"Sure, Ed," I says, and I thought I did, too. I put it down to the ordeal and the hard times the winter had brought his way, that skating was a way he could put all them troubles behind him and just be. But I reckon there was more to it than that, now. "I hear ya. Now you rest up and get better, eh? We need ya good and healthy next season."

"Sure thing, Del," Ed says, though he don't look at me when he says it. Instead, he's looking off over my shoulder, out the window into the dark night. Towards the lake. "I'll do that."

Of course, he didn't do no such thing. Two weeks later, Eddie was dead.

***

"Jesus Christ," Johnsy cursed softly, leaning his head back against the damp cinderblock wall of the dressing room. "I heard about a guy who drowned skating on the lake back when I was in high school. Never knew you guys knew the guy."

"That we did," Barry confirmed, taking a slow step up off the bench to grab a final cold one from the case. He tossed one across to Johnsy before sitting himself back down. "Hell of a guy, too."

"You ain't shitting, are ya, Del?" Johnsy asked, as though I'd string him along with as sad a story as this one.

"No sir," I tell him.

"Goddamn."

The rest of the boys all sit there, saying nothing. Either they heard this one before or they heard enough of it to know how she turns out. I just shake my head slow, take a long pull off my cold one before finishing up.

***

Considering the time of year, Eddie had no business going out on the lake again. Sure, it may have looked frozen solid, but any idiot knows that ain't the case once the snows start melting. Even though there weren't no open water, there's weak spots and thin spots, and Eddie hit one of 'em but good.

Of course, everyone was just devastated. We'd all seen Eddie sliding downhill and it felt like we'd failed him. There was some folks who even talked like it was a suicide. Not that there was ever a note or nothin found. Going out on the ice in the early spring, like he done, don't speak much to good sense, and it does lend itself to the idea that Eddie certainly wasn't in his right mind at the time, death wish or not.

No one knows how long Eddie was out there, striding and looping and gliding across the ice on Lake Manawaka that night, but I like to imagine he was out there as long as he needed to be, taking in the majesty of the cosmos above, at peace with himself and whatever it was that was haunting him right before the crack and splash and the thrashing terror that must have followed. But I ain't so sure that's the case.

Over the years, on those nights when sleep just won't come, I've thought long and hard on Eddie's final season with us. Like how he wasn't himself on the ice, but that the ice was the one place he kept coming back to, hoping to find something. Like how he felt like he was dreaming out there, skating out in the cold. And how the harder he skated, the lighter he felt.

Again and again, I think of the haunted look in his eyes.

They held Eddie's funeral the Saturday after he drowned. All the boys went, of course. Afterwards, we took over the back room at the Legion and got right into it as *Hockey Night in Canada* wound through its double-header. At some point into the second game, after the pints had been swapped for tumblers full of rye, a couple of the guys got talking in hushed tones about some of the grimmer details around Eddie's "death by misadventure," as the local coroner had dubbed it.

Someone driving down the lake road had seen Eddie out there on the ice. They'd hightailed it over to The Dock, where the lounge was still open, pulled in, and got the bartender to call the fire department for him.

"Buddy's just hollerin, 'There's a maniac way out on the ice, skating,'" Hammy, a volunteer firefighter who used to skate with us now and then, was telling the boys. "So we load up and head out. No sign of him when we get down to the lake, but we get set up and soon enough we're out there, working our way further and further from the shore till we come up on it. The hole."

By then, the local Mounties were on the scene, too, cruisers lined up with the firetruck and an ambulance, lights flashing along the shoulder of the lake road. It didn't take them much fishing around before they landed on poor Eddie, hauling his lifeless body up out of those frigid depths.

"It was sad as hell," Hammy says, shaking his head before downing the rest of his rye. Then he sets the empty glass down on the bar and waves for another. "What gets me most, knowing him and all, is that he didn't have no skates on when we hauled him up. No socks neither. Poor bastard was barefoot as the day he was born."

The reason they give for the missing skates and socks? Eddie must have kicked 'em loose as he thrashed about, trapped under the ice and weighed down by his soaking wet winter clothes. Me, though? I don't buy it. No way, no how.

Anyone who ever sat next to Eddie in the dressing room knew the man tied his skates tight as he could stand 'em, pulling on them frayed old laces until he was red in the face. Unless he had the wherewithal to reach down through the deep, dark waters and unlace 'em as he sank, holding his breath all the while, there's just no way those skates shimmied themselves loose. I ain't disputing the fact that those skates were missing when they pulled him up onto the ice not a half hour after he fell through. I just don't know that there's a rational explanation for it.

What do I believe? Well, boys, I've said it before, and I'll say it again: those Bauer Selects Eddie had were haunted, cursed, or worse. By whom or what, I can't rightly say. But I tell ya, they wasn't right.

Come September, as the kids were getting back to school, but before the rink was up and running for the season, I found myself in the sporting goods shop down on Main Street, which at the time was the one place in town where you could find decent used gear. I was looking for some shoulder, shin, and elbow pads for my son, who was just starting atoms at that time. As I was making my way to the back, where the kids' stuff was stored, glancing at the shelves of skates as I passed by, I caught sight of something that stopped me dead in my tracks. My mouth dropped open, slack, and I got a run of goosebumps from my heels up to the back of my head, which was pretty well bald even way back then.

Sitting there on the shelf were them Bauer Selects. They was just as banged up as the last time I seen Eddie lace 'em up, with the swear-to-Christ exact same pair of frayed, mismatched red and black laces that he never did get around to swapping out. The only difference was the blades, which were rusted all to hell. Not, I recalled with a chill despite the balmy weather and lack of air conditioning, unlike how Eddie'd described them when he first come across them Selects himself a year earlier.

"Where'd you get these skates?" I hollered at Jimbo, the shop owner. I couldn't bring myself to touch 'em, to pick 'em up and take 'em to the counter, so I waited, skin crawling, heart hammering in my chest like I'd just got off the ice after getting caught deep in our own end for a long shift, while Jim limped on back into the racks.

"Those rusty old things?" Jimbo says when he finally shuffled up next to me. He scratched at his chin, and his ample belly, mulling it over for a minute. "Couldn't rightly tell ya. Pretty sure they been sitting right there for years."

I opened my mouth to tell old Jimbo he was wrong, but what was I gonna say? That them skates shoulda been thirty feet underwater on the bottom of Lake Manawaka rather than on the shelf of his shop? That he should just up and burn 'em, haunted, cursed, or worse as they was?

No. I didn't say nothin. I just clapped my mouth shut, paid for the gear I needed, and got the hell outta there.

***

Right about then, the old rink rat stuck his head in the dressing room again.

"OK, boys," he said, as he shuffled in and began sweeping at the tape balls and empty cans that had missed the garbage can. "Wrap it up here, for cryin' out loud."

"Sure thing, pal," I said, draining the dregs of my beer and tossing the empty into the bin. It was past midnight and my 6:30 a.m. alarm wasn't getting any farther away. I stood up and stretched, took my coat off the peg on the wall behind me and started pulling it on. I nodded to the nearly empty case next to the trash. "Help yourself there, eh?"

The rink rat stopped what he was doing and shuffled over to the case. After reaching in, popping the top, he stopped to listen, sipping and waiting for the rest of the guys to get up, pull on their own coats and mitts and shoulder their bags.

"Now, I still don't have a hot clue as to how those skates got from the bottom of the lake to old Jimbo's shop there, but I'm sure they did just that," I continued, hoisting my own battered bag over my shoulder. "I seen 'em there with my own two eyes, and even though I'm pushing sixty, I still don't need glasses to read the sports pages. What's worse, I don't know where those skates was before Eddie found them in that exact same spot the year before. But I do know that when the lake's frozen solid, covered in snow as it most often is, and the wind takes to howling something fierce those nights in darkest February, I think of Eddie out there, just skating and skating and skating into the darkness. And then skating some more. And I wonder who or what it was that was pushing him on. I don't rightly reckon I'll ever know. What's worse, I'm not so sure I'd even want to, if I did."

"Man," muttered Johnsy, who was sitting there with his head in his hands. "That's fucked. I'm sorry, boys."

"Don't sweat it," Barry said, stretching before shouldering his own bag. "Let's hit the road here though, eh?"

We all decamped, shuffling through the dingy hall beneath the weight of our bags and sticks, the damp old smell of the rink trailing us out the doors like the ghosts of ten thousand forgotten games. Crossing the parking lot, I waved to the boys before looking up at the full moon shining through the clouds. I wonder, not for the first time and surely not the last, just where those Bauer Selects ended up in the end? I shiver just a little more than the crisp air would warrant, thinking of the cold waters of Lake Manawaka. I hope to Christ I never find out.

Acknowledgements

These stories first appeared, in some form or other, in the following places: "Golf Among Us", as "They Just Want to Play the Game", in *Parallel Prairies: Stories of Manitoba Speculative Fiction* (Enfield & Wizentry); "The Lake Manawaka Meat Lover" on *The Wicked Library* podcast; "Right on the Button" in *Exoplanet* ; "The Coat" and "Ogopogo Lives" in *X-R-A-Y*; "Rock bottom feeders" in *Schlock! Webzine*; "A Lake Wedding" in *Dream Journal* ; "Gord's Still Right Pissed" in *Back Patio Press*; "Shoo Flies" in *Door Is A Jar*; "The Jackalope" in *Bandit Fiction*; "Lyle & Dwight are at it again" in *(mac)ro(mic)*; "X-Files on VHS" in *Flyover Country*; "The Night the Fridge Fucked up Pete's Car" in *Rejection Letters*; "Bauer Selects" in *Alternate Planes* (Enfield & Wizentry); "Good Things on the Way" in *lichen: a literary journal*; "Too Crunchy" in *Sledgehammer*; "The Chasm" in *Bear Creek Gazette*; "The Wind? I Seen it Alright" in *Reckon Review*; "Soo-Soo Go Bye-Bye" in *It Came From the Swamp* (Malarkey Books); and "Dad's Day at the Local Zoo" in *Adam Jeffery Jr. Monthly*. Thank you ever so kindly to the editors who saw something in these words.

Thanks to Alan Good for believing in this collection. Much respect.

Thanks to my wife Clara and my family for putting up with me for so long. I love you all.

Sheldon Birnie is a dad, writer, and beer league hockey player in Winnipeg, Manitoba, Canada.

Coming in 2024

Still Alive, a novel by LJ Pemberton
Thumbsucker, poems by Kat Giordano
Hope and Wild Panic, stories by Sean Ennis
Sleep Decades, stories by Israel A. Bonilla
I Blame Myself But Also You (and Other Stories),
by Spencer Fleury
The Great Atlantic Highway & Other Stories,
by Steve Gergley
First Aid for Choking Victims,
stories by Matthew Zanoni Müller

malarkeybooks.com